Shelby

Translucent Savior

Edited by Steve Soderquist

Cover image by Taya Hardenbrook

This is a work of Fiction. All characters and events are from the author's imagination. Any resemblance to persons, living or dead is purely coincidence.

Special Thanks

I want to give a special thanks to my Editor, who helped make my book come alive. I also want to thank the wonderful group of friends I call my second family; Author and Poet, Ronnie Lee, Author Mistress M, Author Ellie Hart, Author Sarah Mueller and L.W. Michelle. You guys rock!

Mental Illness

"Mental Illness Clouds roll in for my mental storm, waves of fear replace the norm. Trapped in Hell as I scream, internal torment is not a dream. Flashing corpses in a foggy blast, fighting Demons from a haunted past. Lightning strikes and sears my soul, dragging me deeper into this hole. Grasping for a guiding light, tortured memories in the night. Fighting through the pain that's me, a mental monster that we can't see. Talk them up and drug them down, find the surface before you drown. Silent ghouls that surf our soul, shredding hearts as it takes its toll. Mental pain is not our fault, we search for answers from our vault. Cry and rage from deep inside, we need a break let it subside. With the knowledge of our pain, we search and struggle for what's to gain. Crushing sadness is more than blue, you sit and judge without a clue. Spend a day with our feelings, see how fast you start your healing. Our pain is real for none to see, we sit in silence and you let us be. We sigh and shift to push it deep, so you won't treat us like a creep. We're not the same me and you, I'd hold your hand and see you through. I've felt the pain you have no clue, you say its fake and it's not true. You never know what life may bring, just be happy you don't have this thing."

(By Ron Lee)

Chapter One
The Beginning

Shelby saw the old church in the distance as the bells sang a warm welcome with their, *ding-dong-ding* chimes. The morning was gloomy, shrouded in mist, and the air was thick with its dampness. She walked across the newly-tarred gravel parking lot after parking her old gray station wagon in one of the many empty spots available farthest from the entrance.

The church was set back a ways from the old highway. It was small but sufficient for the bantam white church. Capacity seating for the inside was one hundred and fifty at its fullest. The old church, which had been built in the 1800s still held that old Country charm. Just inside the large glass doors to the left sat a beautiful bouquet of newly cut spring flowers; the scent of dianthus and violets inviting her in. The wooden pews with the newly-padded cushions were shouting a warm comfortable welcome. The wooden armrests recently shined to a glossy sheen, were ready for a full house.

This Sunday morning was special. The lady's fellowship group were putting together a nice brunch for all the surrounding farmers and local community... a wonderful way to meet the neighbors, if one were so inclined.

She ambled into the church lugging a basket full of homemade corn muffins and saw the Pastor and his wife standing out front, greeting the folks as they entered. She carried the basket into the kitchen and set it gently on the counter top, leaving them as she made her way to the Sanctuary. With purpose to her stride, she scurried over to greet the young Pastor and his new bride

She waited patiently as she watched the church filled with the worshippers. She scanned the Sanctuary until her eyes landed on them. She hastily made her way over to the third pew from the front and managed to squeeze in beside a younger couple. She smiled shyly and stated just as sweet as apple pie, "What a blessed morning it is!"

Unbeknownst to them of the danger, the young couple beamed at her. They proceeded to introduce themselves along with their two-year-old daughter, Mary Elizabeth.

Chapter Two
The Box in the past

I sat on the top step, swatting at the mosquitoes as they landed on my arm. Sweat steadily streamed down my neck. My eyes darted over the front yard, and I sighed, knowing it was in need of a mowing. Winter was over, and spring was rearing its head with the bursting of flowers, new leaves and foliage, along with increased activity from the wildlife in the outside world. I noticed for the first time all the weeds along the cement walk. Funny I hadn't noticed them before. I twisted my body around and glanced up at the house. The once-yellow house was now a dull tan with peeling paint and torn window screens.

When had the house turned into an old worn shoe? I wondered to myself. My mom kept up on those kinds of things. I twisted back around and leaned back on my hands, stretching my legs out in front; letting them dangle over the steps. The slight breeze cooled my face.

We lived off the main road about two miles down a dirt trail. We didn't have any close neighbors to speak of, and the school bus was the only vehicle beside our own that I ever saw coming down this path.

I was sure glad school had been out for the summer. None of the kids liked me. They all made fun of me, calling me poor white trash. I don't care, really. I would rather be poor than a snob.

The familiar sound of a car coming down the road drove me off the porch and running back into the house, the screen door slamming behind me. I skidded into the kitchen; grabbed the bag of potatoes out of the pantry and set them down in the sink. I grabbed a pan and a peeling knife and quickly began washing and peeling.

"Shelby? We're home! Come and help with the groceries!" Momma hollered when she came in the house.

I wiped my hands on the towel that hung off the refrigerator door handle and went to help with the bags. I skirted around Momma and ran smack into my stepfather, Jack.

"Whoa there kid... slow down," he sneered at me. He grabbed my arm and squeezed tightly, making me wince.

When my mom married Jack, I had just turned five. He was nice to me at first. He would lift me up onto his lap and always hugged me, often buying me new dresses as if on a whim. It didn't take me long, however, to fear him. He got angry real fast.

It wasn't until I turned seven when I realized he wasn't such a nice man. Momma had taken to her bed that day. She was sick with the bug that was going around town. Jack was sitting on the couch, watching the news after supper and had called me over to sit on his lap. He had begun rubbing up and down my leg, his hand slowly moving up onto my thigh. He had slipped his hand under my dress and touched my privates. Trembling, I whimpered and jumped off his lap. I ran into my room.

That had been the first time of many.

I snatched my arm away, running down the steps to grab the groceries out of the backseat of our old maroon Chrysler. I picked up the last two bags and carried them inside, setting them none too gently onto the table. I looked around, wondering where Jack had gone. I was always leery where he was concerned.

"Momma, how did it go today? What did the doctor say?" I asked while taking groceries out of the bags and putting them away.

"Nothing for you to concern yourself with, Shelby." She laid the package of chicken breast onto the counter. "I'm just fine. Now, don't you worry none." She glanced at my face, knowing I was doing just that. She walked over to me and wrapped her thin arms around me and gave a soft squeeze. "I love you...you know that, right?"

I didn't answer. I couldn't get past the lump forming in my throat. I choked back a sob. I felt the moisture pool in my eyes. This couldn't be good. I just knew something bad was going to happen. I squeezed her real tight, feeling comfort in her thin frame.

"Shelby?"

"Yes, ma'am, I know you love me," I mumbled. "I love you, too." I pushed my face into the front of her apron mostly to hide my wet eyes, but also because I loved the smell. She always smelled like a blend of roses and fresh baked sugar cookies.

Mamie Lee pulled away and grabbed a towel off the fridge door. Using the corner of the towel, she dabbed the corners of my eyes.

"Come now, I'll help you. We best get this dinner going." She turned away from me and began peeling the potatoes that I had started earlier.

Dinner was a soundless affair. Jack wasn't saying much, which was odd. He usually bellyached about something. Momma, with that sad look on her face, kept right on eating, once in a while glancing up and looking at me with a sad smile. I smiled back worriedly. I feared what was coming. She was sick.

Momma began going to see the doctor off and on about a year ago. I noticed a change right away. Instead of smiling and laughing all the time, she frowned and would be moody. At night, I would hear her crying softly, but only when she didn't think I was watching or listening. I made an extra effort in helping around the house, although it was getting harder to stay away from Jack's clutches.

One day in particular, I was reading on the porch in my favorite swing when Jack called out to help him in the garage. He needed me to hand him some tools while he worked on the car. Reluctantly and dragging my feet, I did as I was told. When I had walked into the garage, Jack had snuck up behind me and grabbed me, snaking his arms around my middle. He whispered in my ear, "I got you now, little honey."

I cringed and tried to get away, but he held on tight, sucking the air out of my lungs. He was hurting me.

He spoke in the same whisper that seemed tainted with undertones of crawly things that lay rotting in a sewer. "Now you stop that moving around Shelby, and I won't hurt you. I just want a little touch... that's all. Don't you holler none either. Your Momma's sick and doesn't need to be bothered."

I quit squirming and with tears running down my face; I squeezed my eyes shut real tight. Jack had slid his hand down to my stomach and into my shorts. I screeched and twisted away from his dirty hands. I knew it wasn't right; what he was doing.

I started crying. "Stop it, Jack! That's wrong, and you know it!"

"Hush Shelby, your Momma might hear," he chuckled darkly. "I'm a grown man with needs that she can't provide me with no more and soon you'll just have to take her place, I believe. So you shut your mouth now, or I'll make it real tough for you. You hear me, girl?"

I shook my head and pursed my trembling lips, "Just leave me alone!" Terror poured into my soul.

I started to take off into a run, but he had grabbed a hold of my arm again, this time holding me with his hand over my mouth. He pulled me onto the old canvas that he used when he worked on the car. Using one arm and his legs to hold me down, he used his free hand to hurt me.

Mamie's voice carried into the garage, "Shelby? Where have you gone off to?"

Jack swore under his breath and sat up. He pulled me up by my arms. "Go on, get. Don't say anything about this either, Shelby or so help me, I'll hurt you real bad next time."

I didn't utter a word. I wiped the tears off my face and on wobbly legs, ran back out of the garage.

"I'm here, Momma!" I called back as cheerily as I could while trying to keep the tremble out of my voice.

"Come on, girl; I need some help with the laundry."

****

That was just one of many little incidents. I soon learned it was best just to steer clear when he was around. I placed my fork on the edge of the plate. I didn't feel much like eating. The dinner was good and all, but my stomach was pinched in fear. I just knew that my momma was dying.

"Momma, may I be excused?"

"But, Shelby dear, you've hardly taken a bite! Are you feeling well?" Mamie raised her brow and guided her thin hand to my forehead.

"You don't feel warm." A frown marred her features.

"I'm fine, Momma...just don't feel much like eating, is all."

Mamie picked up her fork, "Well...if that's all then yes, you may be excused."

I scraped my chair back and with excited feet, ran up to my room. I fell to my knees next to the twin bed and reached my arm underneath, searching for my most favorite thing in the whole world. When my small fingers touched upon the smooth surface, I pulled it out.

A few years back on my eighth birthday, my momma had brought home a pretty pair of shoes that someone at the church had given to her. It was the first real pair of new shoes I had ever gotten. I had kept the box and decorated it with pretty rocks that I had gathered and collected around the yard. I kept all my favorite treasures inside the box, including all my money. Today, I found a quarter between two floorboards on the porch. I took a quarter out now and put it into the box. I looked inside, and a smile broke out on my narrow face.

I'm saving all my money. One day, I'm going to buy my momma a new house! I knew we didn't have any money right now to buy one, but I would get her one! Why, the only reason she had married Jack was because we needed his money. The house was falling down so when Jack came to live with us; he had fixed it up some. The roof still leaked, however. Maybe if I bought her a new house Jack could leave us alone, so whenever I found a coin or two, in my box it went. Sometimes momma would give me some money if I had to do extra chores.

That went in the box, too.

The lid was my favorite. I decorated it with real pretty rocks. It sparkled from all the shiny white stones. I quickly closed the lid and pushed it back underneath my bed. The bed creaked from my added weight as I laid back and stared up at my ceiling.

I clasped my hands together and laid them near my heart as Mamie taught me and closed my eyes. "Dear Jesus, please help my Momma. I'm real scared she's sick. I don't like Jack much, Jesus, but you already know that. It's just...something isn't right about him. I'm sorry for it, I know he's my step-dad and all but Jesus, he just don't do right. I'm trying to be good, but it's real hard sometimes."

It always seemed to help when I talked to Jesus. I always felt better afterward, like I had just confided to a friend who smiled at me no matter what I had to say.

I rolled over onto my left side and stared at my calendar hanging on the wall. Summer never lasted long. I know I have to make the most of it. Tomorrow I would have to mow the yard and pull some of those ugly weeds. I know Jack isn't going to do it. He never did anything anymore. He stayed in the garage and drank beer most days and only came in to eat and sleep. I don't know why she keeps him around.

Mamie Lee yelled from down below, "Shelby?"

I jumped up off the bed and walked to the top of the stairs, looking down towards the bottom where momma was standing.

"Yes Ma'am?"

"I need to move a few things around and clean my room up. Would you like to help?"

"Sure!" I stepped down excitedly. I was never allowed in her room.

****

Mamie asked an hour later, "Shelby, what do you think of this?" She held up a pearl necklace.

My eyes widened. "It's real pretty!" The necklace had rows of light pink pearls on a gold chain.

Mamie laid the pearls back into the box and closed the lid tight. "Those were my Mother's." she said, smiling wistfully, if not a little sadly. She laid the box on one of the many piles they had made in the room. After a few hours, there were only two large piles stacked up. Mamie grabbed one of the larger boxes that I had piled in the corner.

"Help me put these things in this box, Shelby."

I helped her stack the items, and when that was accomplished, she taped them up and wrote on each one, marking the contents. The tall box, she wrote my name on the lid with a black marker. She turned to me, "Shelby, this is for you. Take this one to your room."

"Yes Momma, I will...but why are you giving all of this to me?"

Mamie sat down on top of the big quilt that lay on her bed. "Because I don't need it anymore. Just keep it in your closet for a while. Now go on, sweetie. Your momma needs to rest. That took all the energy that I had left!" She said, smiling sadly.

I picked up the box, surprised that I could lift it; and even then, just barely. With a grunt, I took the stairs one at time, wincing as the box cut into my arm. When I made it to my room, I placed the box on the floor in my closet, pushing it all the way to the back. I wasn't sure why, but the need to keep it hidden was strong. My closet was sparse, only containing a few items. I didn't like to wear dresses. Only on Sunday's and school days was I made to wear them. I only owned two pairs of shoes. One, a tight pair of black dress shoes and the other, a pair of Oxfords I only wore to school. The rest of the time, especially during the summer, I just went barefoot. The bottoms of my feet were hard and callused, not soft like my mom's.

I washed my face and brushed my teeth, then discarded my clothes into the laundry basket. With one of my momma's old shirts for a nightgown, I crawled underneath the cool blankets and closed my gritty eyes.

I fell asleep instantly.

Chapter Three

Run

The night was almost upon me. I pushed my matchbox car around in circles on the dry dirt. I could hear bells in the background and a woman crying. I picked myself up off the ground in search of the sad sound. My eyes lit upon an old church with white peeling paint. In slow motion, I followed the sound until I lighted upon the front door to the church. Faintly, I could hear someone calling out in a tearful voice, "Lizzy? Lizzy? Where are you?" The sound was made in desperation. A coiled knot of fear twisted inside my stomach. My knees began to knock. A heavy mist formed around me. A door appeared and with a trembling hand, I reached toward the knob. It opened suddenly, and Jack leered down at me, Lizzy?

Shelby?

"Shelby!"

"Uh?" I jerked awake.

It was Jack. "Shelby! Open this door! It's your Mom. You need to come down *now*!" He was hollering from the other side of the old wooden door in a voice I had never heard from him before. It was a frantic, almost panicked.

I gasped in fear, jumping out of my bed and quickly dressed in a pair of cut-off shorts and a white t-shirt. I threw my bedroom door open and flew down the stairs then stopped short, as if I had hit an invisible wall. My eyes widened in shock at the sight before me.

Two men in blue attire were carrying my mom out on a stretcher while another was talking to Jack in hushed tones. I ignored them and ran after the stretcher.

"Momma?" My eyes filled with tears and my heart was beating erratically. I was having trouble breathing.

"Momma?"

Another man also in a blue shirt, pulled me back. "Stand clear, please."

"*NO*! That's my *Momma*! Please, why are you taking her?" Fear raced up and down my spine like chilling fingers.

The blue shirt man gently pulled me back again. "We're taking her to the hospital. Go to your Dad. You can see her at the hospital."

The men loaded the stretcher into the back of the ambulance and then jumped in, closing the doors with a slam.

Bam! Went one. *Bam!* The other.

The slamming of the ambulance doors will always be imprinted in my mind like a burn. Jack directed me to the car, and we followed the ambulance to the hospital. The smell of the place wasn't something I will ever forget.

I sat inside the lobby, waiting to hear something...anything. The clock barely registered A.M. as I yawned, it being a reminder how early it was. I bent over and wrapped my arms around my middle... If anything happened to my momma, I didn't know what I would do.

For the second time in my life, I was truly frightened. Jack wasn't a nice man like my mom thought. Maybe I should have told her about all the times he tried to touch me but I had no place else to go and didn't want momma mad at me, or calling me a liar. I would have given anything to have an older sibling, or at least someone to talk to. I did a quick scan of the lobby seeing it was full of people waiting to hear something about their own loved ones, she supposed. It was sad, really. They all spoke in hushed tones, some of them crying softly and holding each other. I wrapped my arms tighter around myself, me having no one there to comfort me, but me.

I counted the black squares on the floor; every other one being black. I was now up to one hundred and thirty-two, and I stopped, swiping at my face; my hand coming away wet.

I looked up when I heard Jack's voice and saw he was walking towards me along with the Doctor. I watched as they got closer and saw Jack frowning. When we made eye contact, he motioned for me to come over where they both were standing.

"Shelby, the Doc here wants to talk to you. I need to go fill out some paperwork." With that, he turned on his heels and left.

A man in a long white jacket smiled down at me. "Shelby, is it?" At my nod he continued, pointing to some chairs in the far corner of the lobby.

"Let's sit over there."

I followed him dragging my feet. Once we were seated, he faced me.

"Shelby, did you know your Mother had been ill for quite some time?"

I didn't answer, only nodded my head instead. A lump the size of a golf ball had now settled in my airway.

"She had cancer, Shelby...do you know what that is?"

Yes, I know what cancer is, I thought. The lump in my throat increased in size.

I cleared my throat, "Kind of."

"Well...it spread throughout her whole body until it took everything. I've been her doctor for over a year now. She was a fighter. I know she loved you." He paused, then:

"Your Mother has passed away, Shelby. I'm very sorry."

A loud buzzing began in my head. A cramp took hold of my tummy and turned tighter and tighter. How does he know she loved me? Did she tell him that? Why didn't she tell *me* that? Why is he saying my momma was dead? I pinched my arm as hard as I could so I would wake up. There I would see my momma sitting on my bed and then she would lean over and kiss me, and I would hug her. Then we would go downstairs, and she would make me breakfast and then...and...

Instead of my bed, I was still sitting in the sterile and cold waiting room, smelling old people and death. Now I could smell death. It was the worst thing I have ever smelled in my life, and it was all around me.

"But...what will happen to me?" I began to weep openly as everything around me started to pulse in and out, like I was in a mirrored funhouse at the Carnival. Momma took me there once, and we laughed when we saw each other in the warped mirrors...and we laughed and laughed and laughed...

He took my hand, his face gentle. "Your father will take care of you now, Shelby. I know it hurts." The doctor stood up and seemed to open his mouth to say something else, and then closed it and walked away, his shoes echoing off the floor.

My mouth fell open. *It hurts? That's all I get?* This isn't real! I can't live with Jack! Even in my shock at that moment, my mind blew open in panic-stricken terror.

He'll hurt me! I just know it! No!

I felt completely lost now; nothing more than a little fluff of dandelion seed floating loose in a terrible hurricane-force wind. Unsure before, now I had absolutely no idea what my future holds. I watched as Jack moved in closer.

"Come on, Shelby. Let's go home. I need a drink." With that, he walked right past me and headed out through the double doors. I stood frozen for a good minute then on wobbly legs--and with nowhere else to go--I hurried after him.

In the car on the way home, I was nothing but numb. I stared straight ahead at the cars whizzing by, not seeing nary a one.

Jack spoke in almost a jovial tone. "Well kiddo, it's just you and me now." He looked over at me and grinned. Fascinated and in deep shock, I marveled at his silver tooth which seemed to wink at me.

Arriving home, and while Jack was busy locking up the garage and taking his bottles of 'hidden' liquor out to display boldly on the kitchen counter, I ran upstairs to my room. I grabbed my old school backpack and dumped out all the junk it held onto my bed. I crammed my backpack full of clothes, adding a toothbrush and a brush for my hair. My eyes scan over my sparse room. I quickly slide out the box momma had left me, remembering everything we had put in there. I felt physically ill knowing I would have to leave some, if not most of this behind. I opened up the flap and spotted the jewelry box with the pearls inside. That's when I saw it...a large yellow envelope with *Shelby* written on top. When had she put that in there?

I picked up the envelope and walked over to my bed and sat down. After carefully turning it over in my hands, my nervous fingers traced my name. The envelope opened easily, as if my momma knew I would be reading it very soon. I pulled out a sheaf of paper and a folded up wad of money. The letter was addressed to me. I began to read:

My dearest little Shelby,

If you're reading this, it means that I have finally gone on to be with my heavenly Father. I will make this quick. You know how I don't like to write much. I've left you some money in case you need it for anything. It was all I had. I wish I could give you more. The house is yours, but you can't have it until you turn 18. Jack has promised to take care of you, but I don't trust him. I knew what he was trying to do to you, Shelby. I'm so sorry, please forgive me.

19

By the time I had figured it all out, I was already too sick to fight. I have something to tell you, hon. A long time ago, I lived in a small town down in the south of Florida called Laurel Hill. Every Sunday I went to a little country church, and that's when I first saw you. You were so pretty and sweet, and I wanted a little girl real bad. And I couldn't have any children of my own, so I just took you. Your real name is Mary Elizabeth. I don't remember your last name. I have never regretted taking you, and for that I know I will be punished, but I loved you too much for any regrets. As soon, I grabbed you and left, I drove as far away as I could. That's when we came to live in Wyoming. I found our small house and fixed it up for us. I forged a new birth certificate for you. It was so easy, even I was surprised. Made one up on a computer. Take this money Shelby, and get a bus ticket. Don't talk to any strangers. You go find your real mother and father if you want. Get away from Jack. He's not right, and I'm afraid he'll hurt you once I'm gone. I have always loved you as my own, Mary.

Yours forever until time ends,

Mamie xxxooo

I gasped, reading the letter over and over again. I now felt as if my entire life had been ripped in two. One part of me still wrapped in her arms while the other part now invisible. Everything I thought I had known was a lie.

"Shelby? Come down here a minute!" Jack shouted.

Oh no! I took too long! What was I going to do? I've got to get out of here and now, before he comes for me.

With hands shaking, I shoved the money and letter back into the envelope and stuffed it in my bag.

Jack hollered again, 'Shelby?'

"I'm coming, Jack! I'll be down in a minute." I couldn't let him get a hold of me! He was probably drunk by now. My eyes slid to the window as I tried to pull myself together, almost staggering over and looked out. There wasn't any time to think this through.

I slid my window open and looked down. It would probably break my leg if I jumped, but the tree closest to the window was kind enough to offer a few, sturdy branches that I could use to climb down. I hooked my backpack on and had one foot out the window when I remembered my box. I hurried to my bed and fell to all fours, snatching it up. With my bag snug on my back and the box tucked safely under my arm, I crawled out onto the ledge and jumped onto one of the branches of the big oak, quickly scampering down. Once I hit the bottom, I took off in a run down the dirt road, never looking back. I didn't stop until I knew I was far enough away to not be seen from the house. He will come looking for me, I know this...and he will be spitting nails in anger and drunken rage.

I had to reach the bus stop. I didn't have time to try and think about anything else because my mind was nothing but a jumbled mess of disconnected thoughts. First of momma, then the hospital, then the doctor, the letter; everything. When I got on the bus, maybe then I could breathe.

IF, I got on the bus, I reminded myself.

I kept to the side of the road, watching both directions for momma's car. It wasn't long before I heard the familiar whir of the motor. I veered into the woods past the tree lines, so that he wouldn't see me. I hid behind a big pine and watched as the Chrysler came into view. He's driving slowly. I know he's looking for me, but he wasn't going to find me. Never again was he going to touch me! My stomach rumbled uncomfortably, and I prayed he wouldn't stop. It was loud enough for anyone to hear within five feet of me. I tightened my stomach muscles, resolute.

It'll be a while before I get anything to eat. I don't believe I could eat anything, anyway. My entire life has changed. Everything I knew...gone. Momma, why did you have to go?

I stayed hidden, letting the tears fall from my cheeks as I watched the Chrysler slowly move away from me. After the car passes far enough, I began walking again but this time I stayed hidden in case he doubled back, keeping the road to my right and always in my line of vision.

It was late in the afternoon by the time I made it into the town proper. I knew where the bus station was as my Aunt Lilly came to visit occasionally, or used to before Jack moved in. The question was, could I make it without Jack finding me first? I was keeping my eye open to every car that approached or came up from behind me, my heart freezing every time one resembled the Chrysler in any way at all. I try to keep myself hidden by ducking behind trees that lined the streets and between the parked cars. I can smell gas fumes and tar as I bent down on hands and knees, waiting...then getting up to continue.

When I spot the bus station, I also spot the maroon Chrysler right out front. My heart dropped to my feet, unsure what to do. I knew I would have to wait it out until he left, no matter how long that took. I found a 'look-out' spot behind a large tree I was able to peak around it and watch the station without little chance of being seen. I don't hear anyone come up behind me until it's too late.

"Shelby, what are you doing, honey? Playing hide-n-seek?"

I jumped as if I had been electrocuted and turned around to face Mrs. Hendrix, my math teacher from the previous year.

"Hi!" I squeaked. I looked behind me toward Jack's car and my only means of escape from this town.

"Yes, Mrs. Hendrix...that's right! I'm playing hide and seek. I have to go now, so I'll see you later." Mrs. Hendrix's arm wrapped around my shoulder when I tried to run past her to find a more inconspicuous place; it seemed. She pushed her glasses up her nose.

"Shelby, I heard. I'm so sorry to hear about your mom. Are you okay? If you need anything, please let me know, dear."

"Sure, Mrs. Hendrix, I will." Since when did she ever care about me? It made me mad when grown-ups played at caring. "I'm sorry, but I have to go before they find me." I snatched my arm back and sprinted past her. I ran up the sidewalk in the opposite direction from the bus station. I veered to the right, running between two houses. I came upon a gate that was connected to one of the brick homes and opened it, now walking through the back yard until I reached the back fence. I jumped over and took off at a flat-run.

I wasn't sure how far I had gone before I had to stop from lack of oxygen. I bent over, taking in great gulps of air. Once my breathing returned to normal, I glanced around, knowing exactly where my running had led me. I've entered what was called by the locals, *The Black Forest*. There was a legend about the Forest, something about wood sprites living here and such. Supposedly, (according to legend) they protected the forest with magic. It was darker in the woods with tall, thick evergreens surrounding me at every turn. The ground was thick and soft, and my small feet sunk in then pulled out with a soft slurpy sound with each step, but I wasn't about to go back yet. I was simply too tired and hungry. I hadn't eaten anything since yesterday afternoon, and the backpack was heavy, causing my shoulder to ache.

I walked a little further into the dark and eerie woods, the tall trees with their spindly branches seeming to point accusing fingers at me. The rustling of the leaves I was sure were caused from the sprites watching my every move. I shivered and kept walking. There was no way I could go back at this point, anyway...I was too deep in. The legends stated that the sprites protected everything in their woods and now as I was in them meant I was protected, or at

23

least that was how I thought of it. I relaxed my shoulders, pondering on this.

I almost walked right past it, but something caused me to look down, and I saw a hole big enough for someone to lie in at the bottom of a large tree. I fell to my knees and peered in. Nothing but a few spiders. It would be perfect! When a long stick to my right caught my attention, I snatched it up and poked it into the hole, snatching at the cobwebs and making an 'eww' face, removed them.

I pulled the backpack off my shoulders and sat it on the ground, my slender shoulders sighing a thank you. I unzipped it and pulled out a clean shirt, pulling off my dirty one slipping the much warmer and cleaner one on. I wrapped the dirty one around the stick and used it to brush away any remaining webs or spiders. When that was accomplished, I shook it out and wadded it up, placing it into the hole to use as a pillow. It would still get chilly tonight, but this would be a perfect place to sleep and at least keep some of the chill off until morning. I crawled into my makeshift little nest and curled into a ball. I was too tired and hungry to do much else but sleep.

My dreams were fitful; causing me to moan out as creatures of the night came to my unconscious form to gaze or sniff at this strange newcomer into their forest.

Chapter Four

The Black Forest

I woke to the feeling of something crawling up my leg. I opened one eye and peeked down to see and sure enough, it was a black spider. Good thing I wasn't scared of spiders. I brushed it off and crawled out of my hiding spot, the muscles in my arms and legs stiff and sore but not too bad. I stood and scanned my surroundings with my still sleepy eyes. I hadn't been able to get a good look last night.

It was lush and filled with an assortment of greens. The Forest wasn't at all spooky, at least during the day. I brushed the dirt off my legs and arms, deciding it was time to try my luck back at the bus station. Knowing Jack wouldn't be there, this early at least, I picked up my bag and box from beside the tree.

I walked back the way I had come the night before. It didn't take me long to reach the tree line. I used more caution as I followed the same path back into town.

My lips tightened. The car was still parked in the exact same spot. Ironically, he didn't leave. Knowing him, he had probably got drunk and slept in the car. Goose bumps popped up on my arm.

With a heavy sigh, I turned back around. I wasn't even sure how far it was to the next town, and now my stomach was gurgling and growling unceasingly. An old man now occupied the yard with the fence I had jumped earlier, which effectively cut off my last escape route. However, he suddenly got up, and I watched as he closed the gate and walked down the street. I came out from behind a tree and crept back through his yard. I had an idea.

Peering in through his window, I didn't see anybody else. I crept to his back door and tried the handle. I swallowed as it turned in my hand then slowly eased it opened and slinked inside. No lights on, a sure sign no one was home. I spotted his fridge and quickly opened the door and peered inside.

I grinned. Bingo! I snatched out the two cheese blocks, not bothering to read them and a couple bottles of water. I closed the door and looked through a few of his cupboards until I found something of interest. Crackers and a box of ensure breakfast bars. Good enough...they would at least keep me from starving. I stuffed the booty into my bag and crept back outside, looked both ways and seeing nothing, took off at a dead run back into the woods beyond.

Once I was back in the deep of the forest, I slowed my pace. Well, that was half of the day wasted, I thought dismally. What to do now? The way I saw it; I had two options. One, either wait and keep trying until he leaves or two, go on ahead and try and find another town and get on a bus from there. I opted for number two, not being able to be a hundred percent sure if Jack left to just get a bite to eat, only to return fifteen minutes later to find me in a chair, ticket in hand.

I reached the tree that I had slept in the night before and sat down with my back against it. I opened up the bag and pulled out the cheese and crackers. As I ate, my mind drifted comfortably, my stomach thanking me all the while as it graciously accepted the gift.

I spent my whole life in Byron Wyoming; just another small town like so many others where everyone knew each other by first and last name. On one side of the street there was a gas station, a cafe, a bus station, one grocery store, and a five and dime. On the other side, a small library, barber shop and an ice cream parlor. A person could walk up one side of the street and down the other side in ten minutes without breaking a sweat, even in the heat of a Wyoming summer.

My mom kept to herself most days. Sunday was the only day we went anywhere, unless it was for shopping. We got up early and went to church.

None of the other kids were allowed to play with me. I didn't care. I wasn't allowed to interact with them, either. One Sunday, I had overheard one of the parents say, "She might rub off on them." It took me a while to figure out what they meant. Me rub what on them? A loving momma who did her best to make me happy? For the longest time, I didn't understand they meant everything else *but* that.

The crackers and cheese felt heavy in my stomach, settling in like clay as I grabbed a water and took a swig. This town wasn't for me, I decided. It was time I blew this Popsicle Stand; went on to greener pastures...made my own way. I had already made my decision, anyway. I didn't want to think about what came next, but the thoughts came unbidden like summer rain; unexpected and just as impossible to stop.

It wasn't fair! I thought angrily. I had never belonged. She hadn't even been my real mom. Mamie, not my real mom but Mamie the kidnapper. I had a real mom out there somewhere. That thought at least cheered me up a bit.

Excitement burst through my thoughts. *What was she like? Did she ever think about me? Did she love me? Does she have other children? I might have a brother or a sister?*

This was followed by the face of my Mamie...her sad eyes, filled with love for the little girl she stole; the way she hugged and tucked me in, the way she made every birthday special by making each cake from scratch. I was suddenly overwhelmed with feelings of black guilt and prayed to God to please take care of me now, and I was so sorry for thinking bad things about her. In my heart, I knew she loved me, but on the back-end of this, realized that Mamie had no idea just *when* my real birthday was.

After carefully repacking the food, I unloaded my magical box and packed my favorite things inside the backpack. Pausing a moment, I left the box inside the hole for the sprites as a gift for letting me stay and protecting me. I swung the backpack over my shoulder and started to walk away from the town and deeper into the Black Forest.

He watched with glowing eyes as she walked away, quickly and silently skipping to keep up. Chuckling to himself, he shook his head. She wore no shoes on those tiny feet. The girl could have easily blended in like a fairy in these woods.

Within just a few hours, he noticed her begin to tire. It wasn't much further to the small town of Lovell; maybe another hour or two. It was going on noon, and he bet she was about to stop. A few minutes later he wasn't disappointed. He leaned his hip against a nearby tree and watched her. With precision, she picked out a good spot to sit. He was amazed at her endurance and strength for one so small. The girl was thin as a reed, with long, mousy-brown hair that was now tangled with twigs and leaves. She was covered in grime; her clothes stained beyond repair. Yet for all that, she didn't seem to care. If one were to look underneath all the dirt, they would see the real beauty underneath. She was going to be a real looker one day. Her face will bring even the angels to their knees.

It was going to take someone with great courage to travel on this long journey of hers. He had better stay close. Ironically, she reminded him of himself at her age.

My feet were burning something fierce so after sitting down, I rubbed them for a few minutes before taking out the rest of the crackers and cheese out of the pack along with the bottle of water, finishing them off. With just a few drops left of water, I rubbed it into the bottom of my feet, sighing out loud at the cool feeling I wiped my arm across my mouth and wadded up the remains of my lunch and slipped them back into the pack. I was afraid to make the sprites angry if I left my trash in their home.

Time here in the forest was deceiving. With the trees foliage as thick as it was, it successfully blocking out ninety-nine percent of the sun. It was hard to tell where one day began, and the other had ended. With a heavy heart, I stood up and after swinging the backpack onto my shoulders again; I began to walk, completely unaware that I was being watched.

And followed.

Chapter Five

Oreo

I was deep in thought when I heard voices in the distance. It was a man and woman in a heated argument over peanut butter, and I almost laughed out loud before covering my hand over my mouth to stop myself. I tiptoed closer, and my eyes lit up with excitement, as the sun was actually shining through the curtain of trees in front of me. I listened and waited for the voices to fade before I poked my head out and around a tree.

The small town was nestled in a valley with majestic mountains in the backdrop, covered with white snow peaks like covered ice-cream cones. The town didn't boast much, but it was small like Byron only prettier and cleaner. The air had a nip to it coming from the occasional gusts that came down from the mountains, making me shiver. The pair of jeans I had brought would be great about now so I would need to change before venturing out of the protective forest.

I pulled back and set my backpack down, digging around until I found my jeans. My feet were black with dirt and cold, but I figured no one would notice, as they were so dirty they *looked* more or less like shoes. (As long as no one inspected them too close, that is.) I crammed my shorts back into the bag and took a deep breath.

There wasn't much to the small town. The first priority was locating the bus station, which wasn't too hard considering the size. I walked past a little cafe with a sign hanging in the window offering today's specials. I stopped and backed up a few feet, reading it and grinned. A real hot meal would get me a long way. I could spare a few dollars for such so went into the sound of the bell above the door, jingling to my arrival. I glanced around noticing the restroom and made a mad dash in that direction.

I washed my grubby hands in the tiny porcelain sink and looked at myself in the oval mirror. *Oh Cripes!* My hair was a total disaster. I pulled out my brush from my backpack, but my hair was way too wild and tangly for such so combed my hair with my fingers the best I could, pulling out twigs and leaves. I finished by splashing cold water on my face, scrubbing to get some of the grime off and inspected myself.

Not great, I still looked like a homeless waif but at least not one who slept in a tree or something.

The diner was small, boasting only 4 tables and 2 booths for the customers and a long counter up front and to the side of the register. I sat down on a stool at the counter.

A young girl not much older than my own thirteen years handed me a menu and took my drink order. She had long black hair pulled up into a ponytail.

"What will you have to drink, sweetie?" the girl asked, popping her gum.

"Do you have a sprite?" I asked, suppressing a grin as I thought of the Sprites in the forest.

"Sure thing, coming right up. Today's special is a turkey sandwich with a cup of minestrone for $3.99. I'll be right back with your drink." Shelby watched as the girl pulled a red cup out of the stack and filled it to the brim then bringing it over.

"Here you go. Have you decided what you're going to have?"

"I'll just have the special," I answered quietly.

"Sure thing...you want it on white or wheat?"

"Uh... I'll have it on white, please." My mouth was already watering.

"Sure, coming right up." The girl stuck the ticket on a silver wheel and walked back over to me, still popping her gum loudly. "I've never seen you before. Do you live around here or just visiting?"

"I'm just passing through," I said as nonchalantly as I could.

The girl popped her gum and raised her brows. "I would say it looks that way to me. Where are your parents?"

"Visiting some friends," I answered quickly; hating the fact some hick waitress was putting me on the spot in some hick diner. "They told me to come over here and get something to eat so they could visit a while." That was the best I could come up with on such short notice. I thought it better to think up something cleverer before being asked again.

The young girl must have taken my word for it, because she smiled and held out her hand. "My names Betty, my Ma and Pop own this place. I work here during the summer."

I heard a ding behind the young girl. I watched as my sandwich and soup was slid into the window. Betty grabbed up the plate and turned back toward me, placing my sandwich and cup of soup in front of me.

"If you need anything else, just let me know," she said smiling with a gum-pop.

I scarfed my sandwich down in about three bites then ate my soup at a more leisurely pace. After I had finished. I pulled out an envelope and grabbed out five dollars. I laid the money on the table and stood up to leave.

"Hey girl, are you sure your Mom and Dad are waiting for you?" The waitress asked, eyeing my bag. I shrugged. She was nosey, that's for sure.

I glanced away and without answering or meeting her eyes, I quickly made my exit. I didn't want to give the girl a chance to call anybody. After crossing the road, I sprinted back into the forest and then walked, keeping the road in view. I would never catch a bus at this rate. It might not be too far into the next town. If only I had a map! It was probably safer to keep myself to the woods and walk at least for a while longer and now at least my stomach was full. I was still too close to my hometown to feel safe, and my eyes kept darting to the road, ever searching for the Chrysler I had now come to hate. I did know I was at least heading in the opposite direction, and that was good enough for me, at least until I could find a map. I did have a destination in mind, however.

"Oh Momma, why did you do this to me?" I said angrily to the nearest tree. As I continued on, I couldn't help but wonder my real mom looked like. Do I look like her? Would she recognize me if I just showed up like, *Hi Mom! I know it's been awhile! Did you miss me?*

I shook my head and continued on.

****

It had been a while since I left the small town behind. I had come out of the forest after only three days and into a large valley.

I passed an old abandoned building and decided to stop and rest for a bit, plopping down and leaning my back against a tree as I scanned my surroundings. It was pretty here, I nodded to myself. I spotted a field of wild flowers that danced in harmony to the gentle breeze blowing over them, as if they were all in sync to the same music of Mother Nature.

Grabbing my left foot, I laid it on my thigh and rubbed it. I was almost out of the food I had picked up along the way and was hungry enough to eat a whole cow. My eyes landed on something black. A cat, perhaps? I slowly put my foot back and stood up and walked quietly to it as to not scare it away. I walked over to where it lay in the tall grass.

Instead of a cat, it was of all things, a chicken. He was all black except for the few stray white feathers on the top of his head. I was amazed when I bent down to get a closer look. The little fellow

33

didn't move, and I slowly reached out to pet him. His body was covered in soft feathers. He looked up at me with sad eyes.

"*Brock- Brock!*"

"Are you hurt? Is that why you're here?" I asked the sad-looking bird. I picked up the chicken carefully and rubbed my hands all over its tiny body until I found what the problem was. His leg was bent.

"Your momma left you too, huh? Well then, you're just like me. My mom left me, too. I guess we're both broken. You, a leg; me, well...I have a broken heart." My voice cracked a little as I held him up against my chest. I hadn't realized how lonely I was until that very moment. I have never been allowed a friend in school or around the neighborhood, much less a pet. It wasn't allowed, according to Jack. Bad influences and all that. Now I understood that the fewer people I confide in, the more his dirty secrets stayed safe.

"I've never seen a chicken with a top hat on before," I said, giggling a little. That's what the white feathers growing out of his head looked like. "Why, you're the color of an Oreo cookie! I'm going to call you Oreo. Would that be okay?"

When the chicken didn't argue but just seemed content to be held by me, I added, "That's settled then, you're going to come with me. I'll take good care of you, Oreo...I promise."

All of a sudden I didn't feel so alone anymore. I found myself a companion, even if it was just a rather odd-looking chicken out here in the valley for heaven-knew-what reason. Lost, perhaps? Wondered away from his home and couldn't get back and got hurt? I searched in my bag for something to wrap around his tiny leg and finding my old shirt, stripped off a piece. I gathered a couple of sturdy twigs and as gently as I could, wrapped up his leg, wincing with each, *Bock!* he gave me, eyeing me with some reproach now. I shared half of my breakfast bar with my new friend, him gobbling it down in single gulps. Apparently, I wasn't the only one who had been without food for too long. Once all our needs were met, I began walking again with Oreo tucked firmly under my arm, him falling asleep to the gentle swaying lull of my side-to-side steps.

Chapter Six

José

The sun was getting lower in the sky, so I searched to find someplace to bed down for the night before it got too dark to see. I was thrilled when I saw a fence line in the distance. A fence meant there had to be people or maybe even a barn to get into unseen. I crawled through between two warped boards with Oreo tucked safe under my arm. Once I was safely on the other side, I gazed ahead, nodding to myself as I saw exactly what I was hoping for. It looked like an old barn in the distance.

"Well Oreo, let's have a look-see. Maybe we can even find some food if these people keep dry goods in there." I walked as quietly as I could the closer I got, finally ending up almost on my tippy-toes. It was a barn all right; an old weather-beaten barn if I ever saw one and nothing else around it, either. I glanced down at Oreo, who gave me a soft, "bwock", as if he knew to stay hushed, as well.

I whispered, "At least we have somewhere to sleep tonight, huh buddy?" I don't know why I whispered as there wasn't anyone to hear. I crept closer until I stood just inside. It smelled musky of old hay and manure. A little bit of orange light that was allowed shined through the cracks in the wall. I looked for a good spot, and once I found it in the far corner, I looked for items to make myself a nice bed. Sadly, there was no food to be found. What few shelves there were only held some rusted farming supplies and containers of nails, bolts and other miscellaneous items one would expect to find only in the barn. I set my pet down who wondered off to explore, hobbling a little bit as he did so.

"I don't know about you, little buddy," I said to Oreo, "but I don't like the thought of mice crawling all over me, so I need to find us something to lay on besides the smelly ground and moldy hay."

Oreo ignored me and continued to peck at the ground. He seemed content at the moment to inspect everything he could so at least that was something. I quickly scanned the barn looking for anything that might come in handy.

Nothing left in this barn, but rotten hay, I thought as I wrinkled up my nose. Sighing, I gathered up an armful, making a soft pallet. Digging around in my bag, I found one of my shirts and laid it on the top to cover the smell as much as possible. It was almost completely dark now. I finished just in time and settled in, unwrapping the last of my breakfast bar and ate a piece, then gave Oreo the rest.

Using my backpack as a pillow, I lay down and closed my eyes. Oreo would stay close, I knew. He couldn't get far with a bum leg. That was the last thought I had as my stomach grumbled, and my mind drifted into sleep.

****

The boy prodded her with his foot. The young girl was snoring so loud it was making his ears ring with the awful rumble. The little chicken kept pecking at his bare toes, and he thought about eating the varmint but thought better of it. He had seen the girl carrying the ugly thing under her arm last evening. It must be her pet was all he could figure. Maybe she was saving it for dinner. His face broke out in a grin. She might be willing to share with him if he was nice enough. With this in mind, he prodded her again.

"Hey you... little girl, wake up."

I opened my gritty eyes and stared up at the small brown boy. "Who are you?" I asked groggily; startled.

The little boy grinned and puffed out his chest proudly. "My name is José."

I sat up and scooted back against the barn wall. A quick glance in Oreo's direction told me he was still alive. I looked at José' closely. He had on a gray cotton shirt and short jeans. On his arm, was a tattoo of thorns. "Nice to meet you, José," I stammered, not taking my eyes off of him.

"Why are you sleeping here? Where's your Momma and Papa?"

My eyelids felt heavy. "I don't have any...not anymore." I lifted up my chin. "Where are yours? Do you live around here?"

"I don't have any, either. This is my home. I live here,"

"Here? In this barn?" My eyes did a quick scan. The bright sunlight was streaming through the open barn doors now, telling me I must have slept later than I thought. All I saw were more piles of smelly hay.

"I sleep here sometimes, but mostly I stay close by. The hunting is good for rabbits and squirrel. Sometimes I get lucky and catch me a bird." I followed his eyes as they latched onto Oreo.

I jumped to my feet, standing defensively between me and my new friend. "You can't eat Oreo, he's my pet!" I bent down and picked my chicken up and held him protectively to my chest. I raised my brow when I noticed the boy lick his lips.

Squinting at him, I asked, "How old are you, José?"

"I'm fifteen... almost sixteen." He puffed out his chest again.

I blinked looking at the boy carefully. He was so short! He looked more like around seven.

"Are you a midget?" I asked, completely confused but still barely able to contain my laughter.

"No! I'm a dwarf! There is a difference, you know!"

I knew I had made him either angry or embarrassed, by the way his face was turning a deep shade of red.

I smiled wide, attempting to patch up the hole I had just created. "I've never met a dwarf before," I said apologetically as I held out my hand. "Hi José, my name is Shelby. It's nice to meet you."

He put his small fists against his hips. "How old are you?"

"I'm thirteen, almost fourteen," I smirked. He laughed, then held out his hand and shook mine.

"Nice to meet you, Shelby. Are you hungry? I have an extra apple. Later if you want, I can catch us a fish. There's a river down below here that has some pretty big fish in it."

"Really? That would be wonderful!" I hadn't eaten much in the past four days, so the culinary talents of José mattered little to me at that point. The ensure bar had barely sustained me.

38

He turned, and I followed him outside and I saw we were on a hilltop overlooking a small meadow. I barely could make out the river down below us, though I could hear it now as it gurgled its watery path to whatever main river it dumped into. To the left of the barn was a large cement slab which must have been where a house once stood. The land was full of trees and wild flowers and really was a beautiful place, all things considered. Most of the trees were covered in apples. I spun around delighted, an apple orchard! If only I had noticed this last night! I could understand now why the boy stayed here. I held onto Oreo and quickly caught up with him. We walked down to the river together, neither of us engaging in small talk just yet. I kept noticing him stealing furtive glances at me and knew he was sizing me up looks-wise. I smiled a little to myself at his attempts to be coy about it.

José had a pile of rocks set up in a circle. In the center, he had built a fire pit and over that, he laid a long branch across two others like a sawhorse. Some logs were put into place he had fashioned into chairs surrounded the pit. My eyes widened at the ingenuity. He had made his very own kitchen!

"José, how long have you lived here?"

He handed me an apple. He grabbed a long stick he had leaned up against a tree and said without looking at me, "Since the beginning of summer. I ran away from my last foster family as soon as the snow melted."

That had only been a couple of weeks ago by my figuring. "Why did you run away?" I asked, feeling he was a lot like me.

"Well...let's just say I wasn't happy there." He put his stick into the water. He glanced over at me. "Why are you here?"

I bent my head down. "My Mom died. Um...my fake Mom died. I'm looking for my real one." I looked at him, daring him to respond.

José met my eyes, "Oh."

I watched as he pulled the pole back and threw it out again.

"Can I try?" I asked.

"Sure! Have you ever fished before?"

"Nope," I shook my head. "It looks like fun, though."

José handed me the pole and showed me how to throw a line out. He explained to me how to jig and when to pull up. He said I should feel the fish bite. We sat down on the muddy bank and watched the pole. After what felt like hours, but was only about ten minutes or so, my pole bobbed. I felt a light tug. With excitement boiling in my stomach, I hollered, "What do I do? I think I have a bite!"

"You sure do!" José clapped his hands. "Now easy, jerk the pole just a tad."

I jerked the pole up in a quick motion causing José to wince painfully.

"Not so hard, you'll lose 'em!" José stood right beside me now. "Now back up and lift up...gently!" His eyes stayed on the end of the pole as it wobbled back and forth. "That's it!"

I did as he instructed and to my utter amazement, a fish dangled from the line at the end of the big stick. It wiggled around with its mouth wide open, gasping at the alien world it was now thrust into. I jumped up and down. "I did it! I caught one!"

"You sure did! That's good for your first try," José beamed.

He then showed me how to take the fish off the line but took care of the preparations, assuring me he would teach me later. I watched as he cleaned and cut it. He built a fire in the fire pit and strung the fish onto the pole and waited until it was cooked on both sides. He handed me my half, and we sat down on the brittle leaves to eat the spoils of my first victory. It was the best meal I had ever eaten. I tried to get Oreo to eat some, but he was having none of it, instead content to peck around at the seeds he was finding in the tall grass.

After I had finished my meal, I washed my hands in the river. I was splashing water onto my face when without warning, José pushed me in head-first into the cold river.

I came up sputtering and squalling. I swallowed a mouth full of fowl tasting water. I screamed, "*I...can't...swim, help!*" right before my head went under a second time. The cold water went up my nose as panic took hold of my senses.

With wide eyes, José dove into the river forgetting I was twice his size. My head bobbed back up, and I coughed, spitting up water. José was trying to hold me up by my back. He wrapped his skinny, little arms around my neck all the while bellowing in my ear, "Hold on, Shelby! I'll save you!"

I went under a third time the fear so intense now it was causing me to lose focus. I have never been swimming before, but I did know that fear caused worse things to happen. I instinctively knew that if I could just relax and not struggle, I would probably float. I let my body go limp and right before my lungs burst; I floated to the surface, dragging in great gulps of air with José still clinging to me. I tried to un-claw his hands from around my neck.

"José stop! You're choking me," I squalled.

"I'm sorry, Shelby. I'm trying to save you!"

"I'm fine now! You can stop trying to save me." I unclenched his hands and pushed his middle, pulling him off. He fell and slipped under the water for a moment with a small splash. When his head came up to the surface, he started to laugh.

"Look, Shelby, you're standing!"

"Huh?" It was then that I noticed my feet touching the bottom of the riverbed. I felt my face instantly heat up with embarrassment. I could stand up the whole time. It was too deep for José, but not for me. I grabbed a hold of his arm and drug him back to the bank. I sunk down onto the muddy floor just off the tiny shore, noticing I was now a complete mess! I looked like I had been in some un-scheduled mud-wrestling match or something. Oreo came over, gave a cocked eye to make sure it was his human then went back to pecking. I looked over at José, who was now grinning from ear to ear. I smiled and shrugged; resigned as we both busted out laughing.

"At least now your face is clean!" he said between fits of laughter, pointing at me and ignoring the rest of my body and clothes which looked like I had been dipped in chocolate sauce from my crawl ashore. He fell down in a fit of laughter.

After I got out of my wet clothes and changed into dry ones, I rinsed them in the river and wrung them out then hung them on a tree branch to dry. José handed me another apple almost apologetically, which I ate greedily. I lay on my back in the grass and looked up at the sun. It felt good to get the grime off. This was the life I thought as my eyes drifted shut.

I was six or seven, standing in the front yard wearing my new Sunday dress. It was cold, and I shivered.

"Shelby! You stay out here until I say! This is what you get for not minding me!" Jack was looking down at me, and terror filled my lungs, squeezing them painfully. It was so cold! My small feet were turning blue now.

"Do you hear me, Shelby?" He roared, shaking in anger and something else...something dark; forbidden. The monster inside winning the battle of wills day by day by day by...

"Shelby?"

I opened my eyes and quickly closed them again as the sun beat down on my face. I must have fallen asleep.

"Shelby?"

José was looking at me with worry lines etched on his face.

"What is it?" I asked.

"You were screaming," he said quietly.

"Oh, I'm sorry. It was a dream." I turned my head away, not wanting to explain it to him.

I sat up quickly, scanning the area. "Where's Oreo?" I was afraid my new, small friend might have eaten him while I slept.

José watched me wearily and pointed to the right. I followed his hand and spotted Oreo. He was safe, pecking at the ground.

"Geez, I ain't gonna eat 'em, if that's what you're worried about," José said while rolling his eyes.

I smiled sheepishly at his apparent mind-reading skills, and he smiled back, chuckling a little.

Chapter Seven
Traveling Companion

It was time for me to get moving. I felt guilty for wasting half a day as it was. I looked up at the young man before me.

"Thanks, José,' that was fun. I mean, the fishing and all...but I have to get going." I stood up and looked around for my bag. "I have a long way to go before I get to Florida."

I bent down and grabbed my pack from beside me, snatching my now dry clothes off the tree limb and stuffed them in my bag. I walked over to Oreo and picked him up, cradling him in my arms. I turned and started walking back up the hill when José called after me.

"Shelby wait!" He was scrambling up after me. "I'll come with you! You need someone to watch out for the bad men, right? I'm good at that! Also, I can protect you and know how to cook. I'm real good at finding food!"

I stopped and swung back around, eyeing him a bit suspiciously. "You want to go with me? You heard me when I said I'm going all the way to Florida, right? That's a long way. What about your home here?"

"I don't have a home here," he said, expanding his small arms around in a sweeping motion to make his point. "Please, Shelby!"

"José," I said softer now as I noticed his eyes were watering up, "what will you do once I find my parents?"

"I don't know, but I'm sure I can find something to do." he responded with as much dignity as he could muster. His chest that

43

he had at first thrown out at me with such confidence now had a sunken look, adding to his overall smallness.

I thought on it a bit. If he tagged along, I would have someone to talk to besides Oreo. I didn't think he could be much of a protector, though. I looked at him hard. I could see the hope and loneliness in his face shining through clearer than cellophane. I knew that look, because that's exactly what I saw every time I looked in the mirror. It didn't take me too long to decide. Even though I didn't quite trust him, I felt something deep down when I looked in his eyes.

"Okay!" I said. "But you have to help with Oreo!"

José clapped his hands. "Awesome! Just give me a minute while I get my things together." He pointed to the apple tree. "You could grab some of those apples for us in case we get hungry later...sound like a plan?"

I smiled at his enthusiasm. "That's a great idea!" I stuffed some of the apples into my pack as he hurried to the barn and grabbed what clothes and pathetic trinkets he had picked up along the way; things only a teenage boy would find worth keeping, and stuffed them in the old pillowcase he had stolen from a clothes-line a few weeks ago.

José, Oreo, and I made quite a threesome as we walked for mile upon mile, chattering with each other as we began the slow process of becoming good friends. We received a few strange looks from passerby's which we of course, ignored. We slept where we could find some sort of shelter, sometimes even in the trees. José' showed me how to tie a rope around my middle with a knot so I wouldn't fall out when I slept. Most nights, I woke myself up from the nightmares or sometimes José would. He never asked about them, and I never offered. Oreo's tiny little leg was healing nicely. He was walking a lot better now, but I still carried him. He was just too slow or being distracted by some shiny object or another, would start to wonder off. José' helped gather wood for a fire at night, and he was, as promised, good at finding our food. It was nice having help and my respect for him despite his disability, if it

44

could even be called such grew day by day. I knew other boys half his size with less than half his determination and guts. José was the very definition of, 'Don't tell me what I can't do...just stand back and watch me do it.'

The days ran into each other. I wasn't even sure where we were by this point. José' was never quiet, though. He was always talking and sometimes I just wanted to slap him in the face to just shut him up for five seconds, but most of the time I was simply glad he was with me.

It didn't matter how many miles I separated from my home town; I would still catch myself looking behind my shoulder looking for Jack. I would kill myself if he caught me.

"Shelby, we need a map," José said matter-of-factly. "We don't even know where we are or even which direction we're going. I think we've been moving west, but I never finished school, so I don't know my east from my west by looking at the stupid sun or moon...do you?" He looked at me, hopefully, while I scanned my memory to see if by some chance Mrs. Rivers from science had ever covered that. I came up blank.

I shook my head, "No, not really. I vote to stop in the next town and get a map. I have some money," I said.

"You do?" His eyes lit up, making me look at him hard again.

"Yes, I have some, but not much," I answered warily. "How much do you think it'll cost?"

I didn't tell José earlier that I had money mostly because I just didn't trust him enough yet. We must have been close to a town because the traffic on the road had picked up some. I was a little worried about the gray clouds that had formed and were now hovering above us. We were out in the open, and it looked about to rain, and not a little summer rain, either, but a 'boomer' as my momma,

Not my momma my brain insisted like a bug trapped in a jar.

used to say often when it looked like the buckets would need to come out for the various leaks in the roof.

We needed to find shelter, and soon. Somehow we had reached a major highway. I wasn't liking that, either. I didn't think Jack would follow me this far out, but I didn't want to take a chance. Just in case, I had stayed hidden from the roads but now there wasn't anything to hide behind. The trees that had offered shelter had left us behind about a mile ago, and all that stretched before us was the highway, valleys and the mountains far off.

"We need to find shelter, Shelby. Look! It's going to rain," José said pointing to the sky as if I suddenly had gone blind. "Let's look for cover someplace, okay?" We decided to scope out the valley in hopes of finding a farm someplace. By the time we found some sort of shelter, it had already begun to rain. Oreo's head disappeared into his feathers as I carried him. Drops of water ran off my nose, and my clothes were stuck to my skin. I looked down at José and was afraid he was going to drown. We eventually came upon an old drain ditch. It had a big pipe running through it, so we ducked inside and sat down to wait it out.

The rain pelted the ditch, and it quickly filled with water, making this decision a bad one. Lightning and thunder filled the sky, and the water began to flow through the pipe in a heavier stream. We needed to get out before it flooded completely, washing us both to God only knew where this thing led to. José carried Oreo as we made it out and climbed the bank. That was a chore in itself as the constant rain had made the bank nothing more than a mud-slide, and we kept sliding back down, only to try again. I finally made it and helped to pull up José and Oreo. The lightening scared me as it crashed around us in a steady light show, and I was certain I was about to get electrocuted.

"Shelby, look!" José yelled above the thunder. I squinted through the rain at the headlights coming toward us. "Let's try and get a ride!"

What if it was Jack? I would rather weather the storm than face that monster again. I relaxed my shoulders when I noticed it was a truck and not the maroon Chrysler. Jack hopped up and down and waved his arms back and forth, trying to get attention. The truck slowed and came to a stop in front of us. The door opened, and an old man yelled, "Get in!"

We both jumped in the truck and quickly closed the door. Silence met us as the old man glared. His hair was all white; his face weathered with bushy eyebrows to match.

The man pulled out slowly, watching the road through the heavy downpour that seemed to have no intention of letting up. "What in all that is holy are you young'uns doing out in this storm? You lost or something?" I didn't know what to say, but José did.

"No, sir. We were catching butterflies when the storm caught us instead. We're sure glad you're giving us a ride! My sister got scared," he hooked a thumb at me to drive the point home. "Oreo here was sure to drown, too!" He grinned wide, showing his crooked teeth. I exhaled slowly and slumped back into the seat. I reached for Oreo, who suddenly decided to speak up with a loud, "Bock!"

The old man guffawed, "Well, you sure wondered off a ways from home. It's about nine miles to Cheyenne. Is that where you two live?" he asked.

"Yes, sir." I spoke for the first time. I was learning to lie. The heat from the truck was making me tired.

"Well, it's going to take about thirty minutes to get there in this weather," the man said. I leaned my head back and closed my eyes. I could hear the tiny splats of water dripping onto the floorboard of his truck.

"That's fine," I mumbled. Then amazingly, dozed off.

Chapter Eight

The Fight

When we reached the town of Cheyenne, the rain had all but stopped to a light drizzle. We thanked the old man after he let us off at the first stop sign. José told him we lived just around the corner. He waved and drove off, leaving us to wonder still where to get a map. This town was much like the rest we had passed through; small, a tiny strip mall and about all of one traffic light. I spotted a gas station, and we headed in that direction, first needing to get out of our wet clothes. I could only hope what was in my bag stayed fairly dry. Looking at José's sad ragtag pillow case, it was obvious it was as drenched as he was. Well, maybe I had something not so girly I could loan him for now.

The gas station was small with only two rusty pumps and signs hand-scrawled in the window that looked faded and yellow, as if they hadn't been bothered with for years. The red sign flashing through the window glowed 'open.' I walked in and asked the toothless guy behind the counter if I could use his restroom. He handed me a key on a stick and pointed outside. I thanked him and walked back outside, taking José in tow while digging through my bag.

"I will be right back," I told José.

The restroom was small, with just one toilet and a small sink stained a reddish brown. Water dripped continuously from the faucet, and I quickly changed into a pair of dry clothes. They were dirty, but a lot better than wet. I quickly did my business and washed up as well as I was able with no mirror. I took out a ten and a twenty-dollar bill for later and stuffed everything back into my pack. I met José out front.

I pulled out a shirt that had an AC/DC logo on it and handed it to him.

"Here, change into this. At least it's dry. I've got nothing you could use for pants, though," I finished a bit apologetically.

"No skirts?" José said grinning at me. I laughed a little... apparently, being wet did nothing to dampen his sense of humor.

"I do, but you'd be prettier than me then!"

"Nothing is prettier than you," he said, then turned quickly away heading to the restroom, but not before I saw his cheeks burning a scarlet red. I sighed, knowing he had a crush on me. Girls could always tell when a boy does. It's written all over their faces like it was in bright, neon paint. I sighed again, wondering if that would complicate matters in the future.

When he came out replenished in my shirt, I tugged at his arm lightly. "Come on, let's find a map and maybe we can get some food." I took Oreo out of his arms, and we went back inside the station. I asked the attendant if he had any maps. Without speaking, he pointed to a rack full of different maps.

I whispered to José, "Which one do we need?"

"Well, since we're going to Florida, we better get the whole United States map," he answered, nodding his head at his own, wise advice.

We both decided on a map showing all the detailed routes then went in search for something to eat. I found a bag of mixed nuts and fruit for Oreo, then grabbed some jerky and crackers and added a couple of candy bars and soda. José did the same, adding to our small pile of booty. I gulped my sprite while the attendant told me in a bored tone the total was seventeen dollars and fifty-four cents. I didn't realize how much stuff costs, never purchasing my own food before in a convenience store. Mamie always paid.

"Wow, dude! Where did you get that kind of money?" José asked me as we left. I looked at him and shrugged, and he only nodded, not repeating the question. If anything, my new friend knew the art of others discretion.

We found a perfect spot at a small Park in the center of town. A cement path led to some benches with trees adorning all sides giving us at least a bit of cover from the town's main road. Wild flowers grew in abundance around us, giving me a sudden sense of nostalgia from taking walks in the part with Mamie in the spring. We found a spot and sat down to eat, both of us ravenous as we tore into crackers, cheese and snicker bars, both of us making audible, *yum* sounds as we munched. I let Oreo roam on the ground and watched as he pecked at his treat.

"My Mom left me some when she died," I answered suddenly with a mouth full of chocolate. I loved chocolate. I couldn't remember when the last time I had actually eaten any. Candy at my house was a rare treat.

"How much did she give ya?" he asked, looking at his candy bar and not me.

I eyed him suspiciously. "Why are you asking?" I wasn't going to tell him...not yet anyways. "I don't have much more." I finished, perhaps a bit too quickly, by the way his eyes sharpened as he started at me.

"I'm not gonna rip you off, Shelby," he said now, his voice reflecting some hurt. "I don't want your money, okay?"

I was about to apologize to him when goose bumps popped up on my arms. I shivered and glanced around. Two older boys and a girl about my age were watching us. José followed my stare and glanced over.

"They look like trouble to me, Shelby. Let's go."

"No, José, we aren't bothering anyone. Besides, my feet hurt, and I like it here". I wearily watched as the trio walked toward us. The girl was dressed in a pair of shorts that sparkled and a half shirt that showed her belly. The boys wore jeans with holes in the knees. They were cut on purpose, I observed...not like mine that were worn thin and in places all but tatters. The tall boy had shaggy black hair while the other was chubby with a short-cropped buzz-cut. I straightened up with half my body stiff. I watched Oreo from out of the corner of my eyes.

"What are you two doing in our Park?" the tall boy asked, crossing his arms and looking down at me while the chubby one moved in closer to José'.

"This isn't your park; it's a public park." I told him, not showing any fear.

The girl moved in closer and snarled, "This is our park, and we don't allow trash in it!"

José jumped up. "We aren't bothering anybody, leave us alone."

The girl started to laugh hysterically. "Look, Jimmy, it's a midget!"

Something in me blew like a volcano that over-heated. I didn't think; I just attacked. Everything that had happened to me in the past few days that was always close to the edge exploded in rage as I grabbed the girl's hair and yanked her down onto the ground and jumped on top, punching her in the face.

I heard her call out as if from long distance, "Stop!"

I didn't stop. Swinging my arms back and forth, using my fists on her face, I kept hitting her. I felt myself being lifted up, and suddenly I was flying through the air. I landed hard into the park bench. I heard a crack, and sharp pain raced through my side. I shook my head and started to get up.

"Stay down, dog!" The boy spit and stepped on my left hand. He bent down and lifted my head up by my hair. His fist landed a solid blow to my left eye. Lights flashed behind my eyelids as my head exploding in murky stars. He let go of my hair, and I slumped to the ground. I felt the pressure of his shoe leave my hand and then it connected with my stomach. I grunted. I couldn't breathe. I heard one of them holler, then the sound of running feet echoed in my head. Bile rose up in my throat and gagged me. Pain, sharp and fierce pounded at my face.

José was on the ground, holding his nose. I stood up painfully while holding my side with my arm and went to help him up. Blood was pouring out of his nose. I needed to find something to stop the flow. He was bleeding all over my shirt now and was generally nothing but a mess. I went to grab my bag, but it was gone. I quickly scanned the area. Oh no! I fell on my knees, retching violently in the grass.

"José, they took my bag! All my money was in that bag! Everything I owned in my bag!" My mind exploded in panic. They could have the money, for all I care! All could think about now were my Mamie's things she had given to me that were in it. I swung around and looked in the direction they had run. No sign of them anywhere. I couldn't help the tears that ran down my face unbiddenly. Everything I owned was gone. Every piece of me that even hinted at my existence and my Mamie's...gone. The necklace she had given me, the money; my clothes and the rest of our food. I would never be able to get on a bus now. All I had left was eight dollars in my pocket and the crumpled up letter Mamie had written to me. I bent my head in shame. I had wet my pants. I sat back on my heels and cried harder.

All I could think about was what were we going to do now? I had nothing but the dirty and now smelly clothes I was wearing, my chicken, (who thank God was still here, pecking away as if nothing had happened) and a companion who had beaten up because I couldn't control my temper... I was embarrassed and utterly ashamed.

José sat down next to me. "Shelby," he said softly through his plugged up, poor nose, "It's going to be alright. Listen, I have an idea. Have you ever heard of the Salvation Army or Goodwill?"

I nodded my head, "My Mom, I mean Mamie used to shop for us there."

He wiped the last of the blood off his top lip. "Well, we can see if they have one here and if they'll help us. They help people, right? We could get some clothes and maybe get you a new bag. Come on, let's go look."

I shook my head, feeling pity for myself. "I can't, José. It's not the bag... it's what was *in* the bag." All I wanted to do was hide. My side throbbed something fierce. Pain shot through me every time I took a breath.

"Why not? They'll help us; I know they will!"

"I can't!" I hollered, then felt instantly contrite and petty; just a little girl throwing a tantrum. I might as well have thrown myself on the ground and started kicking my feet in the air.

"I'm sorry," I said, more subdued now but still crying, now in mortified embarrassment. "I can't because, I... well..." I bent my head, my hair covering my face. "I wet myself, José.'"

It was silent for a few minutes. I peeked at him through my layer of hair and saw he was sitting on his knees; anger etched onto his face. At first I thought he was mad at me until he said, "I should have fought them harder, Shelby. I'm sorry. I wasn't much help."

"There were three of them, José!" I exclaimed angrily. God help him if he had fought back harder. They probably would be talking about a hospital instead of the Salvation Army.

José nodded his head. "Yea, maybe...come on, let's find a place for you to hide until I can find you some clothes. Don't worry...I won't say anything." With that, he suddenly leaned over and pecked my cheek, his face glowing more than it had when he called me pretty, and then dashed off to search for a quick place for me to hide.

****

Later, I sat huddled in some bushes just outside the park. I could hear other people walking by, but no one could see me. José had once again delivered on his promise. I had to smile a little. If anything and despite his size, he was fiercely protective of me. My eyes teared up a little, wondering what I had done to earn such loyalty from such a gentle soul. I waited for José to get back, and I could smell my urine strongly as it wafted up, making me crinkle my nose. It was difficult to breath, and my left eye was swelled almost shut. I lay down on the soft mound of grass; so tired now. I was so tired. My eyelids were heavy, and my eyes felt gritty. I soon became oblivious to the pain in my side and drifted off to a troublesome sleep.

****

Jack stood at the end of the bed.

"Wake up, missy girl! It's time to play with Daddy!"

"No!" the girl cried from under the blanket. "I don't wanna play tonight. I'm tired!"

"Shush now! We don't want to wake up your momma, do we? We both know how sick she is. Don't be a selfish little brat."

"No!"

"It'll be fun! We'll play, 'I touch, you touch'. Ready, Shelby? Shelby?

Shelby!

****

"Shelby! Shelby? Shelby!"

"What?" I mumbled at José. I sat up disoriented, the pain coming back immediately.

"Hey, I found you some clothes." He handed me a brown sack, which I eagerly grabbed. I dug in and pulled out a pair of faded jeans and a blue t-shirt.

"Wow, thanks!"

"I spotted those kids across from the Goodwill store where I snagged these. We need to get out of here. Let's get to the next town and then find some more clothes and stuff. I don't want those kids coming back."

"No."

José looked at me and blinked. "No?"

"No. Not without my bag."

"Shelby, it's just money...we can find more," José said cautiously.

"It's not about the money," I stated firmly. "There's more in there that's a thousand times more valuable to me. Money won't replace it!"

"Okay, okay!" José said, seeing he obviously wasn't going to win this argument. "Well, we need a plan."

"Plan or no plan, I'm getting my bag back," I said with a growl.

José shrugged and shook his head. "Okay, c'mon then. I swear, either you're really brave or a bit of a nut."

We found them just where José said they would be, hanging out in front of the closed store. I saw my bag at the girl's feet as they talked, her still nursing her wounds from the beating I had administered to her.

"Okay," I whispered. "As soon as they start to leave, we'll---"

That was as far as I got before my eyes widened seeing José slinking through the bushes towards them.

"José!" I whispered harshly after him.

If he heard me, he completely ignored me. Stunned, I saw him creeping up to a town patrol car parked about a block away. The cops inside were dozing, apparently bored with another night in their tiny town and catching up on rest.

José picked up a good size stone and aiming like a pro ball-player, winged it as hard as he could, smashing it into the cop's car rear window and cracking the glass. The two cops inside jumped, startled, as the teenagers looked on with mouths gaping open and scanning the area to see where it came from.

"Hey! You three, stay right where you are!" One of the cops bawled. The teens did as they were told, paralyzed with fear. I could see and hear everything as the cops walked briskly towards them.

"Let's see those hands up! Now!" The cops now had their hands on their side arms. Obediently, six hands shot in the air as if on marionette strings.

"Who threw it?" The larger cop barked at them.

"None of us did...sir!" tall-boy gulped. "I swear!"

The smaller of the cops, (who by definition was really not small at all) was studying the girl closely.

"What happened to you?"

"She fell," came the immediate response from crew-cut boy.

The cop whirled in his direction. "I didn't ask you... did I, pudgy?"

"No sir!" he squeaked.

"Well, lookie here, Sam," The larger cop said, holding up the hands of tall-boy, "bruised and bloody."

Officer Sam inspected the hands of crew-cut boy now. "Same here, good buddy."

He pulled the teen roughly around and got out his cuffs while the other did the same with his own suspect.

He looked hard enough into the eyes of the teen to make him shake. "I guess they like hitting on girls...what say you, Mike?"

"Looks so to me," Mike drawled, nodding darkly.

The girl spoke up. "They didn't do it! I swear! We saw some other kids in the park and we..."

"Shut up!" tall-boy hissed at her.

She shut her mouth immediately as Sam the cop consoled the girl gently. "It's okay, honey. You don't have to be afraid. We'll get you someone to talk to."

All the while, José had snuck around one of the few, parked cars near them and was now reaching for my bag.

"There he is!" crew-cut boy suddenly cried out, spotting him. "There's the kid who threw the rock!"

The cop spun around while my breath caught in my throat like a snare. Almost magically, José shrunk himself even smaller and made himself disappear behind the rear tire of the car.

"Nice try, kid...get in!"

Now both handcuffed, the teens were stuffed in the back of the patrol car while the girl was placed in front. As crew-cut and tall-boy turned to look out the window, they saw José swinging my backpack on himself, then turning around...he flipped them both off with his middle fingers, a huge grin on his face.

I could see their mouths first drop open, and then shouting obscenities only they could hear, and I finally couldn't help myself. I rolled back as tears of hysterical laughter burst out of me, making my side ache even more but I could care less.

José was back within a minute. "Here ya go! Merry Christmas from Santa José!"

He smiled widely and plopped my bag down beside me, and I couldn't help myself. I jumped up and grabbed him up in a huge hug, lifting him off his feet. José made an *Ooof!* sound as his breath was all but squeezed out of him.

"Thank you!" was all I could say.

For himself, José had not a clue what to do with a weepy, hugging female so tentatively he hugged her back, hoping that was the right response.

"Umm, you're welcome," he managed.

I set him back down and kissed him soundly on the cheek.

"That's for taking care of me."

José blushed three more shades of red, unable to meet my admiring gaze. "Anytime," he mumbled.

In a way, he hoped her bag would be stolen again so he could retrieve it.

I pulled some fresh clothes out of my backpack and rooted around; relieved beyond words the box Mamie had given me was still there and not surprised in the least to see all the money gone. I quickly changed while José waited for me on the other side of the bushes.

I left my old clothes lying in a pile, and we left the park at fast as our legs could carry us. Oreo had made it through the whole episode unscathed. I held him against my chest, rubbing my hand back and forth across his feathers.

We were quite a pair, with bruises and swollen faces. My muscles were stronger from when I first began carrying Oreo. I could carry him longer than before. José carried him some, but mostly I did. Oreo seemed content sitting in my arms and being carried around like a little prince or something. He was a curious little fellow who now watched every move I made as if keeping an eye on me. I grinned to myself, thinking I now had *two* bodyguards of the least likely variety.

Even when I set Oreo down he followed close. He sometimes still pecked at my dirty feet, (when I took my shoes off, that is...José had made sure to find me a pair when he went clothes diving at the Goodwill drop-box) but mostly when he was hungry. I guess it was his way of communicating. His feathers were soft, and I often rubbed my hands over them, both of us finding enjoyment in this.

"I wish I could take a bath," I told José' a while later as we walked. I could still smell the urine on myself and by now was making me feel ill to my stomach. If José smelled me--which he had to--he did a darn good job of acting like it didn't bother him in the least.

He grinned crookedly, "I heard two old men talking when we were in the store about a lake up the road where they go fishing. I don't know how far it is, but we'll need to find a place to sleep tonight, anyway, so let's see if we can find it."

"That would be awesome!" I smiled. Just thinking of jumping in a nice, cool lake was enough to make me hurry my steps along.

When we found it, (it wasn't hard...as soon as the ground got mushy I knew we were close) I saw it was more of a pond than an actual lake. It was murky and muddy, but I didn't care...at least it was wet and had to be cleaner than me. I didn't have any clean clothes to change into so I asked José if he could stay back while I washed some. After discarding all my clothes and leaving them to hang on a nearby brush, I planted Oreo on the ground to be my watcher and jumped in, my body immediately gulping in the cool water. I grabbed some dirt from the bottom and scrubbed my skin as fish jumped to the left of me. Maybe José could catch us some to eat later. It was a little difficult to get my arms over my head. Each time I moved, sharp pains lanced through my side.

José never said anything, but I knew my face must be an ugly sight. A large discolored mark was left on my stomach. After I had finished scrubbing with dirt to get the dirt off, I went and grabbed my clothes and put them on. I was wet but didn't care. At least I smelled better. I whistled to José that it was his turn.

I wandered around in the fading light looking for a good spot to sleep for the night. We needed to be hidden in case someone happened by. It was warm tonight and for that I was thankful because I had nothing to cover myself up with when I went to sleep. While José was finishing up his own cleaning, I collected twigs and leaves for my pallet. José found me a few minutes later and was carrying an armload of branches he had foraged for.

He dropped them, saying seriously, "I think we could safely build a small fire. I found a long stick I could make into a pole to fish with, as well." To prove this, he showed me by almost poking my eye out.

"Good deal, José," I said grinning; thinking a patch over one poked-out eye would match my bruises just about perfectly. I giggled, hiding it behind my hand.

He dropped his pack on the ground and dug inside. He pulled out some string and proceeded to string his makeshift fishing pole. Once he put the hook on, off he went back to the pond.

José caught three bass. They were small but good. José sat down on the hard ground, expertly cleaning the fish with his small pocket-knife.

I watched him, admiring him more and more. "Where in the world did you learn to do that?"

He looked over at me and grinned. "My family never had money...for food or anything, really. So my daddy taught me to do this by the time I was three."

I nodded as he went about his work. I sat down across from him in front of a small fire he had gotten going and touched my cheek delicately, hissing at the pain that seemed to bloom outward wherever I touched it.

"I've seen worse," José said, talking about my eye. I grinned at him as he scooched a little closer to me. He reached over to put his arm around me.

"Don't touch me!" I shrieked. "I hate to be touched!" Faster than a cat that had let its tail in the fire, he pulled back and stared at me.

"I'm sorry," I said defensively. "I just don't like to be touched, is all."

"Why?" he asked, a bit mystified considering how she had hugged him earlier.

"Why what?" I shot back.

"Why don't you like to be touched?"

"I just...don't. Drop it, okay?" I stood up. I wasn't sure why his question irritated me, but I was suddenly angry enough just to haul off and punch him right then.

"Sure, no problem," José said stiffly, going back to the fish and skewering them now on branches.

After we ate and put out the fire, we both fell into our makeshift beds, Oreo tucked by my side.

"I'm sorry, José."

I heard him sigh as he rolled over. "It's okay. I guess you'll tell me when you're ready. I won't ask again, alright?"

"Thank you," I said, crying a little and hiding it so he wouldn't hear me.

Within minutes, I heard his soft snores and rolled over from the glow of the fire. I wished and prayed with everything I had that I wouldn't dream tonight.

But I already knew I would anyway.

Chapter Nine

Daniel

I woke up just as the sun crept over the horizon. Oreo was asleep, snuggled against my outstretched arm as I took a personal inventory of myself, stretching a little and took a sharp breath, moaning. I was sore and stiff as a board; my eye swelled completely shut. I sat up and looked around with my one good eye and saw José curled into a ball with his thumb in his mouth making him look more completely like a baby. I stood up and went to splash water on my face at the pond, and when the cold water hit my face up my nose, I fell back on my bottom, sputtering. I caught my breath and held it, then let it out slowly. I stood up on wobbly legs and plopped down in front of an old pine tree, trying to let some of the hurts and kinks work themselves out...I wished I had remembered to pack some aspirin or something. Oh well.

It wasn't fair! This kind of thing only happened to other kids, not me. My chest suddenly felt heavy and my heart so overwhelmed I cried. I had lived with a woman who, kidnapped me and took me from my real parents then raised me as her own with a pedophile pervert. She then had the nerve to get sick and die on me when I was at my most vulnerable. How could someone do that? Thinking back, it wasn't just Jack who didn't want me to have any friends...it was Mamie as well. I understood somewhat why now. Someone might have found out about me and called the police. What hurt me the most was the fact she knew jack was hurting me and didn't do anything about it! Now, here I am stuck in the middle of nowhere with a flapper jack and a chicken, all because of her. I hate her! I have no money, no clothes, I'm hungry, and on top of all this, my stomach began to cramp...perfect timing for that little visitor...not! I balled my hands into fists and pounded the ground next to me. Tears rolled down my face and landed onto my hand, glistening. I watched as the tiny drop rolled off. The worst part was I missed her in a way. The one person who I thought I could trust and love. She was actually a criminal, and now all I could think of was my warm bed back home. I sobbed loudly, covering my face with both my hands, sure I was going to wake the dead with my bawling, but I just couldn't stop. My side hurt, and the more I cried, the worse the pain, and here I was calling José, a baby!

He stood behind a tree, silently watching her. It broke his heart to see her cry, but he had no idea how to comfort her. His first thought was to go to her and put a reassuring arm around her, but after last night's fiasco of the boy doing that, he thought better of it. The tree supported his lanky frame as he leaned his hip against it. He crossed his arms over each other and listened to her wretched sobs until he just couldn't take it anymore. He pulled away from the tree and came to a halt in front of her.

"Please stop crying. Everything's gonna be okay!"

Startled, I held back a scream and suddenly stopped crying. I looked up and around for José...he sure could sneak up on a person, no doubt there...but the voice didn't belong to José.

"Who is that?" I said jumping up now and turned in a circle, my eyes searching the dense, wooded area.

"Oops, sorry about that," he chuckled.

Right before eyes, the boy appeared. One second he wasn't there then the next, he was standing right in front of me.

My eyes grew wide as I pushed my back tighter up against a tree.

"Who are you?" I asked the boy now, suspicious. "And how did you manage just to appear out of nowhere?" I leaned sideways and peered behind him to see if he was alone.

"Easy," the boy replied.

"If it were so easy then I could do it."

"It's easy for me, Shelby." He bowed his head "My name's Daniel, at your service!"

"I blinked back my surprise. "How did you know my name?" I looked closely at him; he was tall with a thin frame. The contrast of golden hair and sparkling blue eyes caught my breath despite my fright, and a fluttering began in my belly, making me blush a little despite my earlier scare.

"Oh, well... I heard it when you and José were arguing," he said matter-of-factly.

Daniel looked down curiously and laughed when Oreo tried to peck at his bare toes. He bent down and picked up my chicken, remarking, "Why, she's just lovely. A Polish game hen, in case you didn't know. They do make the best of friends, don't they?"

I watched as Oreo took to Daniel. I held back a smile. If he was nice to animals, I figured he couldn't be *all* bad. He did talk a bit funny, though. I mean, what boy used the word, *lovely*? I tilted my head and squinted down at his feet. I laughed out loud then quickly covered my mouth with my hand. What if he was like the others?

"What's so funny?" he asked, smiling a little.

"Your sandals. I thought only girls wore sandals."

"I like sandals; they add comfort to my feet." Daniel sat Oreo back down, and I watched as my newly dubbed prize hen wobbled slowly over to a pile of old leaves, pecking for breakfast.

"You said a game hen?" At his nod, I continued, "So 'he' is really a 'she'?"

"Yes," he said.

I relaxed my shoulders. "Do you live around here?" He shook his head without going into any further explanation.

I wiped my hands over my face. I knew for sure I was a mess. Snot running down my face from the cold water; my hair a wild and tangled mess, my stolen clothes, which were ratty to begin

65

with now suffused with caked on dirt and rips. I grabbed the bottom of my t-shirt and wiped off my nose. I wanted to crawl into a hole in the ground and disappear.

If Daniel noticed my embarrassment, he didn't show it. "By the way, don't say anything to José about my little appearing trick Shelby...only you and Oreo need to know." He dropped a conspirator's wink to her, a sparkle in his eye.

"Why?" I frowned, immediately suspicious again. What was he hiding?

"Because I may need to do it again sometime, that's why," he shrugged.

"Were you following us? Where did you come from?" I eased myself up and glared at him, not one to be intimidated; or at least *show* I was intimidated. Truth be told, by this time I jumped just about every time I stepped on a crackling twig. A thought suddenly occurred to me. As crazy as it was, I felt it needed asking.

"What happened to you? I mean... are you a ghost or something?" I felt stupid asking, thinking on the heels of that that if Oreo could see him, then he must be real.

He laughed a full belly roll, "No Shelby; I'm not a ghost. It was just a trick."

"If you're not a ghost, then what are you? How did you do that?"

"I can't tell you," he winked.

I felt my face light up. If it *were* some sort of trick, then I would love to learn it. God knows it would come in handy not just for me, but for José as well.

"I can help you guys." Daniel said now a bit more serious.

"Help us?"

"Yep. I thought I would help you find your mom. That *is* where your destination, right?"

66

I cocked my eyebrow. How did he know that? We made eye contact and as I saw the kaleidoscope of swirling colors of blue I felt I could simply melt in those eyes.

"How do you know all this stuff?" I asked?

"You mentioned it when you and José were arguing," He repeated patiently, motioning towards the small camp José and I setup last night. "I overheard it."

I didn't trust this kid at all yet, thinking he must have been following us the whole time. He did seem nice, though...even if he was more than a little bit odd.

"So you want to come with us, I assume?" I asked, already knowing the answer.

He nodded.

"Well, I need to talk to José first." I said, wondering how in the world my fierce little protector would cotton to such a prospect. I instinctively knew José's first reaction will be jealousy. I sighed...

"Have some faith, Shelby. You're going to be fine. Don't you feel better already?" the strange boy asked.

What an odd thing to say! However, I did feel better just in knowing someone was willing to help me. José wasn't much help against the enemy on a one-to-one basis, but his cleverness made up for that. I realized I wasn't upset anymore. I didn't think he would hurt us, something in his eyes told me that. I dusted the dirt and leaves off my clothes. I looked over to where Oreo was sitting. He began to squawk loud. I jumped.

"Oreo, what in the world are you bellowing about?" I demanded. Maybe chickens have a sixth sense about evil. I glared at Daniel. I was ready to tell him to get lost.

"Don't worry, Shelby...she's just laying an egg," Daniel said smiling.

Chapter Ten

Friends

José glared up at me. "We don't even know him, Shelby. What if he tries something?"

"Like what, José? I don't have anything he can steal, and you don't either. I'm sure he can't fit in your clothes." I added smartly. "I didn't know you, either," I said with hands on hips. "He's taller than me, for one and might come in handy in a scrap... also he..." I bit my tongue on the last, knowing I almost shared Daniel's little disappearing-reappearing act.

"Besides, what if he doesn't have a mother or a father or nowhere else to go? You know...like us!" I was trying to be patient and rational, but talking to a teenage boy about a potential competitor for a girl's attention was likened to knocking down a building by kicking it repeatedly.

"He's probably just lonely. To tell the truth, I think he was hiding out here when he saw us," I finished.

José was clearly un-convinced. "What if he's a killer on the loose and the police are looking for him or something?"

"He doesn't look like a killer to me and he's your age, José. You think a teen murderer would be hiding out in woods and talking to people like us? Besides," I finished, wondering a little to myself just why the heck I was defending someone I had barely met so passionately, "He's really skinny." *And cute.* I felt my cheeks burn. I decided to wisely keep that one to myself. José was watching me closely. Okay, so he is cute, but that wasn't the only reason I wanted him to go with us.

"And?" José said now, knowing there was something I was holding back.

"He's probably hungry!"

José muttered and scowled at his feet.

"We're going to need all the help we can get. We're lost and don't have any money. I don't know what to do."

José turned away from me and grabbed his bag. I watched, waiting for him so say something. I wanted him to agree that we could use the help, and we couldn't do this on our own. Truth be told, I somehow felt safer around Daniel. He seemed harmless enough and after getting jumped by those hoodlums... well, the more the merrier, I say. I felt more than a little mean thinking we would be less likely to get jumped again with someone like Daniel around, but there it was. I wanted José to agree, but if he didn't, I was still going to let Daniel tag along. José could just be mad at me and deal with it; I didn't care. We needed the help and everyday I was falling in deeper over my head. I watched as José stomped away; then he turned back around.

"Fine, then! Come on, and bring your new *boyfriend* along, too." His short legs marched away. I sighed and shook my head a little, then hollered for Daniel to hurry up and follow. José had taken about twenty steps when he turned back around and snarled. "He can carry Oreo!"

Oreo? I had almost forgotten my buddy! When I looked back at Daniel, he had already retrieved Oreo. He held out his hand. I tentatively walked over and looked. In his hand was a small, white egg. I gently plucked it out of his hand; fascinated that my chicken had made this. He smiled, and I swear his teeth sparkled. This boy had the whitest teeth I had ever seen. We walked on, eventually catching up with José.

I have to admit, we made quite a sight walking together...a tall blonde-haired boy in sandals, a midget with a chip on his shoulder, one chicken that laid eggs and pecked everyone's feet, and then there was me; the rag-a-muffin leader. I felt liked a warped Dorothy on some twisted, yellow brick road on her way to see the wizard. I wondered how many witches and evil warlocks we would encounter on the way.

I imagined quite a few.

****

By mid-afternoon, the sun was hot and beat down on us. We had been walking for the better part of the day, and my feet were crying for a break. I stole glances at Daniel every so often who never seemed to tire...or sweat for that matter. I was practically dripping, and I noticed José was as well. Daniel wore light-blue cotton pants with an even lighter blue t-shirt. For once, I envied his sandals. José and I still looked like the Raggedy-Ann couple with the only addition to José being the same scowl he wore on his face since we left our little camp this morning. I was getting tired of his sassy attitude, to tell the truth. I was hot and hungry enough to eat a grizzly bear.

I raised my head up and shielded my eyes with my hand. The sun was finally heading back down. It was approximately around two or three, by my guess. I needed to rest, and my stomach cramps had taken a turn for the worse. My period was about to start and not for the first time wondered what was I going to do. It's not like there were sanitary napkin dispensers along the sides of roads; as well as knowing even we did see a gas station or store, I didn't have the money to buy any. It was times like this I hated being a girl. Why couldn't boys have a period? They didn't even get boobs, which almost hurt as much when they started growing! It just wasn't fair. God must be male, was all I could figure, harrumphing to myself a little

My pants were sticking to me now as I pulled my shirt away from my sweaty skin and blew down the front. José still hadn't spoken to either of us. I halted and glanced around for a place to rest. Daniel also stopped and waited by my side. He sat Oreo down. I brushed my hand across my forehead. I thought the heat was sure to kill me long before my cramps started to sing in full choir. (My periods were always expeditions into hades.) It must be 100 degrees out here. I hollered for José to stop.

"Buzz off!" he hollered back.

I had enough of his sour attitude. No one said he was, or could be the boss, anyhow. I stomped up to him and glared down on top of his dark head.

"That's it, José! You can either grow an inch or go on your own. I'm tired, hungry, about to start my period and am sick and tired of your attitude! Daniel is with us, so get over it! Do you hear me?"

"Fine by me!" he snarled, marching on.

My eyes widened. I swallowed hard. Oh no, what have I done? He can't go by himself! I hate this! I balled my fists up and jumped when I felt a hand on my shoulder. I relaxed and let out a sigh.

"Let me try to talk to him. It's me he doesn't like," Daniel said. I nodded.

Daniel was right, of course. While he went to speak with José, my eyes searched for a place to squat. My bladder was full to busting. Trees lined both sides of the road. I looked down the barren highway, and I could see what looked like steam rising off the black top. I headed in the direction of the nearest tree, one that was big enough to hide behind. I grabbed up dead leaves from the ground and hid. After I finished my business and was about to stand, I noticed the blood run down my leg. I didn't want to cry. Not in front of the boys. I used the rest of the leaves as padding. When this was accomplished, I stood on shaking legs. I didn't want to go any farther. I needed rest and something to eat. I noticed the boys were waiting for me and watched José's face for some sort of clue as to his disposition and didn't see the scowl anymore, at least. I smiled at them both.

José lowered his eyes and kicked at the dirt. "I'm sorry, Shelby."

"Thanks, José," I gave him a small hug which he cringed from a little...waiting for me to go Jekyll-Hyde on him again, I supposed and sighed. "Hey guys, can we find a place to rest somewhere around here? I need to rest, and maybe we can find something to eat." I looked at Daniel not thinking, "Hey, do you think you could find us some food?"

"I'm sure I could scour us up something." he replied

"No! I mean, that's my job, isn't it Shelby?" José said, obviously offended.

"Yeah, José, it's your job, too," I said apologetically.

"Don't forget about the egg. Also, Oreo popped out another one a few hours ago...see? Daniel held another small egg in his palm. "We could scramble them, I suppose."

"Um...I don't know if I can eat her eggs," I said, my face a little green at even the idea.

José grinned, "Eggs? Oreo laid eggs? That's so cool, Shelby! Wow, I'm glad I didn't eat her after all."

I glared at him, "Yeah, whatever! Where is she anyway?"

"Over there," Daniel pointed. Oreo was wandering around, pecking at the ground. That's about all that the chicken did. Sometimes she thought my toes were something to eat. Her beak was hard. It hurt something fierce when she pecked at them, but I let her anyway. To me, she was just another reminder of the antithesis of my life rolled into one, big mess.

Peck! Peck! Remember, you're a kidnaped child! Peck Peck! Remember, there's a pervert still chasing you! Peck!

I sighed heavily.

"Come on, let's check the place out and find a place to rest," José said, leading the way.

We followed José off to the left of the road. We wandered about half a mile through heavy thickets of brush, he being able to navigate them easily while I was being whipped and snagged at every turn, making more holes in my already ragtag clothes. Neat-o. Daniel seemed just to glide through them without a care in the world. I looked back at him hard, and he just smiled, which only served to anger me for some reason. We came across a small clearing and made a place we could all rest. José dug into his bag and came up with his trusty hook and off he went in search of a river or pond of some sort. Daniel went to go collect some sticks for a fire while I rounded up some pine and leaves for a soft bed. Once that was accomplished, I lay down and closed my heavy eyelids, immediately falling into one of my familiar nightmares.

I couldn't breathe. It hurt.

"Ah Shelby, you are mine, aren't you?"

"Please stop," I moaned. "Please stop. You're hurting me." I turned my head toward the right. With tear-blurred vision, I saw momma standing in the doorway watching...

A shake. "Shelby?"

I jerked up, as always thankful to be interrupted but as always, drained more than refreshed.

"What is it?" I rubbed my gritty eyes. I glanced around, and it took me a minute before I realized where I was. "I fell asleep."

"Are you alright?" Daniel was bent down on one knee, watching me, his face emotionless.

"Yes, I was just real tired is all. How long have I been asleep?"

"Not long, about thirty minutes. José caught a squirrel." He nodded to the right.

José had a squirrel skinned and on a stick over a fire. And on a rock beside the fire were two eggs cooking.

"How are managing to cook eggs?" I asked Daniel, impressed. The eggs were sizzling, and the scent was heavenly, despite the source that still made me feel a tad queasy.

Daniel smiled. "We heated the rocks, then just cracked the eggs and walla! Fried eggs! Your dinner will be served shortly, ma'am. Sorry, we didn't find any water nearby but we have a little left. At the very least, we have this mini feast!"

The food smelled wonderful. My stomach growled noisily, and an embarrassed flush rose up my cheeks. When the squirrel was finished roasting, José served us each a portion of the juicy meat on a leaf. We split up the two fried eggs evenly three ways. After all the food was gone, we took a vote and decided to stay the night and start early in the morning. José guessed we were about a half a day's walk from the next town. When Daniel went to explore, I pulled José aside.

"José, I need a change of clothes and I need some...girl stuff. Do you think goodwill would help me? I mean, could we find one in this next town, do you think?" It was one of the hardest things to ask. I could feel my face flush.

José nodded his head and didn't need to ask about girl things, not that he would in a billion years, anyway. "Oh yeah, I'm sure of it. They have them in all the towns. They have them to help people, Shelby. Do you need me to go in and ask for you? I know you're trying to keep a low profile and all that."

"No!" I exclaimed, blushing even harder at the thought of a boy who looked about eight going in and asking for tampons. "I...um, no I can do it this time. I just don't want them to call the law or anything like that. Do you think they would do that if I go in there and there's like a poster of me or something?" I've never heard of a place just giving clothes away to kids...at least not without them wanting to know about the parents, I figured.

I voiced my concerns to José, who nodded wisely. Apparently, he had been around this particular rodeo a few times.

"They ask, but you just have to come up with a good lie, is all. I do it all the time...and no, it's not the post office, Shelby, and you didn't rob a bank or anything, ya know." He shrugged his shoulders as if it was no big deal.

That was good enough for me. I walked back over to my makeshift bed and lay back down, full and contented now. I burped healthily which kicked up my ribs, which were singing a new hurt-tune again seeming refreshed by the nourishment in my belly.

Chapter Eleven
Thief

We made it into the next town right before five PM. We hid Oreo behind an old barn on the outskirts of town knowing that we would draw enough attention as it was from strangers without us carrying around a chicken, to boot.

José stopped and asked a gray-haired man where the Goodwill was located. He gave José directions and handed him a five-dollar bill, obviously noting his ragged appearance. José handed me the money and told me to get my girly stuff. I think he knew what I needed. I couldn't meet his eyes.

The store smelled of mothballs and old cigars. I wasn't sure what I was supposed to do or where to go, for that matter. The whole place was a mish-mash of racks that seemed to make no definite sense beyond the thin half walls separating the clothes from the books and electronics. Daniel wasn't shy though, walking right up to the counter and asked for someone in charge. A nice old lady came out from the back room, and after Daniel had explained our plight, she nodded sympathetically and told us we could pick out two outfits a piece, including socks, shoes and undergarments. I was so grateful I wanted to cry. I was sure she saw the moisture in my eyes because she gave me a look of extra kindness. However, I hated pity more than anything else and my cheeks burned. I grabbed José's hand and made my way down the aisles, grabbing a pair of jeans, Capri's shorts along with two t-shirts. I was ready to get out when José reminded me to get the under-things and shoes' while they were free. I found a comfortable looking pair of walking shoes and some sturdy ladies underwear, and when I had everything, I walked over to the lady and asked her about the female stuff. I could hardly get the words out without biting my cheeks. She smiled and led me to the back of the store into a restroom. She opened up a drawer in the bottom of the shelf and brought out a couple of packages.

"Here you go, honey. Let's find you a bag so you can carry these, shall we?"

I followed her gratefully over to where a collection of backpacks hung on the back wall. I grabbed the nearest one and stared down at my toes.

"Thank you." I couldn't look her in the eye. I just knew I would bust out crying if I did. "Thank you, for everything," I stuttered out. She smiled gently and gave me a little hug which I returned. I almost burst out crying again smelling her soft, lilac perfume that reminded me of Mamie.

I waited by the entrance door for the boys to finish shopping. Daniel was taking his sweet time. Inspecting every item like a bomb-expert, turning it this way and that; holding the item either up to his chest or at his waist to check the size. I was rocking back and forth on the balls of my feet and tapping my toe at the same time. José came up behind me.

"Did you get everything you needed?" he asked.

"Yes, I did." I handed him back the five dollars. "I didn't need this. We should use it and get more water and snacks and another map." He knew ours had for whatever God-knows reason was stolen by the hood teenagers.

"If you say so," he shrugged. He pointed to my bag, "You got a new backpack? Cool. Are you feeling better now?"

I didn't know exactly how to answer that question. I couldn't answer him because honestly I didn't know myself. Was I better now? Better how? I wasn't better. I didn't believe that I was ever going to get better. I leaned my back against the wall and watched as strangers walked by holding hands with their children. Better?

Never! Could it get worse even? Well, that may be yet to come. I made a non-committed gesture to José that told him nothing.

Daniel came out whistling and swinging his bag. "Hey guys, sorry it took so long, but I couldn't decide on blue or brown?" he grinned.

I looked at him, just shaking my head. Did nothing phase this guy? He spoke up as we left the store. "Where to now?" His eyes moved back and forth between us.

"Well," I said slowly, "we need to find another store first so we can buy a few essentials like water, and snacks case the umm...wildlife gets scarce, and also another map."

Daniel nodded, "Sounds like a good plan. What about showers? Maybe we can find a park somewhere with a fountain or something?"

Both José and I gasped at the same time, remembering well our last experience in a public park.

"*No!*" we both said emphatically at the same time.

"Okay then... I guess that's out," he said rolling his eyes.

"We don't like parks, is all," José frowned.

We walked around until we found a small convenience store. José and I went in while Daniel waited outside, watching over our bags. I walked over to the row of maps, trying to find one similar to the one we had before. When I found it, I walked over to the counter and after paying for it along with a gallon of generic water and three candy bars, (that was all the five would stretch for) I asked the man behind the counter if he could circle the town where we were in, making him give me the old hairy eyeball of suspicion but I didn't care at that point. If anything, I wanted to bite out that if his crappy town had at least a streetlight that didn't dim every time someone plugged in a hair-dryer, I might have been able to find it myself and thank you very much. Instead, when he did this for me, I thanked him and stuck the change, all whopping thirty-five cents into my back pocket. The map was cheap but still cost more than I thought it would, but I was thankful the kindly old man had given the money to José in the first place, or we would've had nothing. I borrowed his pen and took a moment, unfolded the map and located, Laural Hill, Florida and circled it, then traced the route in what I figured the most direct way from where we were. When I turned to leave, José was already gone.

"Look what the man did." I pulled out the map and showed the boys. "He circled the town we're in for us, and I circled our destination. Come on, let's find a good spot to sit down and figure it out."

José was fidgeting something fierce. "Great! Come on you guys, hurry!"

I noticed he kept looking toward the store entrance; it worried me. I folded the map and placed it into my back pocket, and we just started to cross the road when I heard the store alarm start blaring.

I looked back, completely baffled. "What's going on?"

"*Run!*" José yelled.

"Wait, José," Daniel grabbed him by the back of his shirt just as he was about to take off at a run.

"What's going on?" I asked confused.

The man from the store, the one who had circled the town on my map came running out of the store, pointing at José. "Stop that boy! He's a thief!"

José wiggled out of Daniel's grip and took off running. "Wait, José!" Daniel called.

"*Stop!*" The store man screeched as if he was just robbed at gunpoint.

Now there were sirens, and a police unit came into view. A car pulled up alongside us.

"What's going on?" Daniel asked the officer when he stepped out of his car.

The cop eyed them dryly through his mirror glasses. "We got a call from Mr. Johnson the store owner that a young boy stole a few things out of his store."

"No, he didn't!" I said indignantly. "He was with me the whole time! He didn't steal anything; I just bought a map and some snacks!" The nice gray-haired clerk didn't look so nice now as I turned to him. "José didn't steal anything! I have the receipt, right here!" I shoved it in front of the officer's face, my fear of Jack temporarily forgotten. Stealing was a crime, and they could take José away from me.

"Then why did he run?" the officer asked me, a small, tight smile on his stony face.

"Probably because you scared him," I said, gritting my teeth.

Daniel shook his head sadly.

I raised my eyebrows. Did he believe the store-owner's story? José didn't steal anything! He was right beside me the whole time!

"Where do you kids live?" the policeman asked as he pulled out a notepad and pen, paying too much attention to my discolored eye.

I gulped. I glanced over at Daniel. I shook my head in a silent plea.

I noticed the cop looking me up and down. He pushed his glasses up a little as I heard the squawks issuing from the radio pinned to his large chest. "Do you live around here?" He directed his question towards me again.

I shook my head. People were beginning to stop and stare. A small crowd was gathering; a bunch of nosy busy-bodies that had nothing better to do this morning, I supposed. I wasn't surprised in the least. I wanted to scream at them to go take a hike somewhere else. The only time people minded their own business was when someone was hurt and actually needed help.

"Where are your parents?" the cop asked, persisting. He paused a moment, saying something into his radio, waited for a response, then said something else. The whole time, he rooted me to the spot where I stood with his presence as effectively as if he had glued my feet there.

I could feel myself starting to panic. I stepped back a step. The cop was asking too many questions and now was reaching behind him. That told me only one thing... handcuffs. I think Daniel sensed it. Without a word, I took off at a dead run, Daniel right on my heels. All I heard was, "*Hey! You stop right there!*" I ran as if my life depended on it. Heck, my life *did* depend on it. I knew where José would go, and that's where I was headed. Oreo would be with him, as well. I ran and ran. I didn't stop. Dodging in-between cars, I tore down allies and in between houses, not even bothering to look back to see if I was being pursued. I crawled under a fence and kept running until I thought my lungs were about to burst. My legs felt like rubber when I finally made it back behind the old barn. I dropped down to my knees and sat back, taking in great gulps of the moldy and stale hay-filled air. José was sitting cross-legged with Oreo on his lap, watching me carefully with wide eyes.

Daniel came in behind me. I had heard his tread before he spoke. "José, did you steal from that store?" he asked harshly.

I immediately saw red. I jumped up and turned, facing him. "Are you accusing him of stealing too, Daniel? Huh? How dare you! You don't even know him! He wouldn't do that!"

Daniel didn't even look at me. He was watching José.

"Yes, I would, Shelby." I heard José say softly from behind me.

I stopped dead cold. All the anger suddenly dissipated as quickly as it had appeared. I slowly turned my head around and stared at José, feeling sick inside.

"What? What did you say, José?" This is unbelievable. I give him a sharp look, narrowing my eyes.

"Yea, I stole," he repeated.

"Why? Why would you do something like that? Do you realize what almost happened? I would have been caught, and they

80

would've made me go back to him! Do you know what he would have done to me, José! Huh? Do you? *Do you?*" I balled up my fists at my sides.

"Shelby, stop it!" Daniel yelled. He splayed his hand on my shoulders, sensing I was about to leap on José and beat him to a little pulp. I let out a deep breath shakily.

"Why?" I asked José again, a bit calmer.

"I was hungry, and I just wanted a candy bar," he cried.

I shook my head. He wanted a candy bar...a stinking candy bar. Of all the childish, stupid...

"I *bought* us some candy bars, you nit," I snapped out.

"I'm sorry, Shelby, I really am. I didn't think about it. I just did it. I didn't think we had enough. And we only had five dollars, and needed a new map and... please don't be mad at me." His eyes were welling with tears now.

I glared at him. He was such a baby sometimes. I felt so much older than him. Were all 15-year-old boys like this? I wondered. I sat back down beside him. My ribs were on fire. It hurt to breath.

"If you *ever* do something that stupid again, I'll turn you in myself, buddy!"

"Okay," he mumbled. I watched incredulously, as he unwrapped a Hershey candy bar and broke it in half. "Do you guys want some?"

Daniel shook his head, "No thanks, I don't really like chocolate. You two go ahead." He sat down on the other side of José. "I think it would be a good idea if we hole up here for a while. Maybe head out when the sun goes down."

"Yeah," we both agreed.

We waited until the lights went out all over the town. Daniel suggested we wait even longer, but I was anxious to leave. If we stick to the outskirts of town, maybe we could bypass it all together. We walked through the night mostly in silence, each of us in our own little world. Even Oreo was quiet.

****

The following morning when we came upon a small lake, we hid behind some trees and looked around for any movement. A log cabin stood on the other side with a long dock running out from the front with a boat tied to the end. I eyed the lake with longing, to just jump in and wash some of this grime off of me. I would give anything to feel clean again. I could smell José a mile away, so I was sure he could smell me. I raised my brow as I glanced over at Daniel. He looked the same as when I first saw him. How did he stay so clean? He didn't even smell. I was seriously in need to put on some fresh clothes and get out of these jeans. Coupled with that, I could feel the stickiness between my legs. Without a word, the three of us--Oreo included--sat down and watched for movement. When my leg began to cramp, I stood up.

"Listen guys, I don't see anyone around. If we're real quiet, we can each take turns and watch out for one another. I'll go first." I said, not giving either of them any choice in the matter.

I crouched low and half-slid, half-crawled down the embankment. When I reached the water's edge, I looked back up to see if the boys could see me. When I didn't see them, I slid off my bag and took out a clean set of clothes. I peeled off the smelly ones, my face wrinkling in disgust as I saw my thighs were covered in streaks of blood. I hastily made my way into the water and with a hand full of sand and rocks, scrubbed my body as best as I could. I dunked my head in, my scalp tingling at the refreshment offered. It felt wonderful to get the grime off. I quickly finished up, changing into the clean clothes and used a tampon the lady had given me. I rinsed out my dirty clothes then made my way back up the embankment. I could hang them out the next time we stopped for any length of time.

"Who's next?" I asked, coming into the clearing relaxed and fresh.

José went first and took longer than I did, making me want to chide him about never saying how long it took girls in the bathroom again for the rest of his life. After he had returned, Daniel went down, but I got the strong impression that he was only doing it for show. In less than five minutes, he returned...looking almost exactly the same, the only difference was he had at least bothered to get his hair wet.

I shot him a curious look to which he only smiled in return, saying nothing.

We traveled at night and rested during the hottest part of the day. I was a little frightened at first, but soon became used to the quiet of the dark. I found that I could walk much faster with my new shoes as the rocks didn't cut into my soles, or that I didn't have to keep my eyes solely on the ground looking for anything sharp enough to cut me. We tried to find places to rest that had water nearby. Sometimes, strangers were helpful and other times they were just down-right mean.

It didn't take me long to learn the difference between good folks and bad ones. The good ones had sparkles in their eyes. They were always quick to smile. I learned quickly to watch faces for these signs. The bad ones had a permanent frown etched onto their foreheads as if they were branded by the scowl-police. They rarely smiled, and their eyes were dead to anything and everything that didn't benefit themselves in some way or the other. I wondered what the stories were behind those eyes. Were they like mine? I wanted to ask Daniel if I had sparkles or if mine were dead.

I was afraid of what his answer might be.

José and Daniel became fast friends, more like brothers. They watched out for each other. We all watched out for one another, for that matter. I came to rely on them more and more. What started out as the mostly unlikely of misfit pairing was now more like a tight team, each of us by now knowing what the other was thinking without hardly a hesitation. We slept beside each other, snuggled for warmth together, (Daniel often with his arm around José protectively) hunted together and shared together. Everything we had, we split evenly three ways without a word. I reflected that no matter what my life may hold in the future, this would be the parts I would look back on with the most fondness. I felt both blessed by them, and terrified at the same time I would lose them. I don't believe I could have made it this far without them. If José didn't find something for us to eat, Daniel did. My job was to provide a place to rest and help with cooking and scavenge for supplies.

I pulled out the map every day. We had outlined a route to Florida, Daniel saying we needed to get there before winter. None of us knew how long it would take to reach it. Daniel said it was about 2000 miles or so. Once in a while, we got lucky and were served hot meals at a town's local church. Some of the folks gave us food wrapped in tinfoil, and they never asked us questions. Those were good days.

I wish they had lasted longer.

Chapter Twelve

The Snake

"What's the next town, Shelby?" Daniel asked. They were currently in Colorado and had stopped for a rest, as it was the hottest part of the day and learned not to push it, lest we lose more miles than we gain. The Rockies surrounded us on both sides of us like giant sentries forever at their posts. It was pretty here and we all remarked on how impressive our surroundings were.

"It looks like a real big one here," I said, pointing to the blue star on the map marking Denver. "We can go this way though and go through this little town called Tulip."

We agreed unanimously to stay away from the big cities as we had found out most were nothing but trouble. More often than not, the odd stares and questioning looks was enough to put all of us on edge. We always knew when we were close to a city by the heavier traffic. When this happened, we left the main roads and hid in the tree lines, waiting for breaks in traffic or just following along out of sight. I was always watchful; forever in the back of my mind that Jack could very well be somewhere still out there, hunting me. It was cooler in the trees, anyway. The highways often gave off a heat enough to roast a pig, even at night. Spiders and creepy crawlies hid in the trees and only seemed to come out during the evening, though...and that wasn't okay with me by a long shot. Even with all the miles we had put in, I was still very girly-girly about this despite the half-hearted chiding by my traveling companions.

"I smell water," José stated excitedly. "Come on."

I would have scoffed at this if I didn't know better. He had a nose on him like a beagle, and he has proven it more than a time or two. I glanced at Daniel and smiled knowingly. He grinned back. My breath hitched. Every time he smiled at me I got this fluttering feeling in my stomach.

We followed José through some trees about a half a mile and sure enough, we soon ran into a beautiful stream that ran east and west against the mountain. It was a breathtaking view. Large boulders sat adorning the bank on either side of the running stream like they have probably done since time began. "Let's go for a swim!" José was already peeling off his shoes.

Daniel cleared his throat, "I wouldn't advise it, José. Not now, it's too dark."

"So?" I exclaimed. I wanted to go also.

I wanted, no needed to bathe again, (it had been three days) and get some of this road-dirt off of me. I looked back a little defiantly at Daniel, my eyes telling him the dark wasn't going to keep me out of the water, either. Besides, the moon was bright with a perfect round of the full moon. It wasn't as if it was completely dark, we could see just fine.

"Come on, Daniel, it's still light enough." I followed José and took off my shoes. I waded out into the stream and it wasn't even deep. It only went to about above my knees. The ice-cold water felt soothing on my feet. I dug my toes into the sand and I grinned wickedly, bending over to scoop some water up into my hands and splashed José, who was still standing by the bank. The water would be up to his chest where I was standing, and I knew he wouldn't dare to come out this far...or maybe he would, knowing him. I watched in horror as he dived in with his clothes still on. Drat! I sometimes forgot he can swim like a fish. I squealed, and walked-half ran out of the water before he caught me. Daniel sat on a boulder laughing. When I reached the bank, I was laughing so hard that I didn't see it.

Daniel screamed, "Watch out! Snake!"

I felt a sharp pain shoot instantly into my ankle. It felt like a bee sting, but instead of disappearing, the pain got steadily worse. José was quick and had the snake caught up by its head. He grabbed up a rock and smashed it, then swung it into the blackness beyond.

"Sit, Shelby!" Daniel ordered. He was beside me in an instant, helping me onto the boulder he had just vacated.

"Let me look." The snake had bit me just above my ankle bone. "José, get me your knife, quick! Then build a fire."

Daniel took off his pack and grabbed one of his shirts, ripping off a sleeve and tied it around my ankle so tight my foot began to tingle. José had a fire going in no time and stuck his pocket-knife into the flame without being asked. After a moment, he handed the knife to Daniel, his small face all eyes in his worry. I watched with horror and could only think over and over, *Please Daniel don't cut off my foot! Please Daniel don't cut off my foot! Please, please, please!*

I squeezed my eyes shut.

I hadn't realized I was repeating my mantra out loud until Daniel glanced up at me as tears welled up and ran down my face.

"I'm not going to cut off your foot, Shelby. I need to cut a slit across the bite so I can get the poison out," he reassured me.

"Let me do it!" José demanded. "It's my knife!" Daniel looked back at José; a silent agreement must have been made because Daniel nodded and stepped back. He held out the knife to José, who cut a long slit across the two holes and then quickly bent over my ankle and began sucking out the poison. I scrunched up my face. Ewe! Every few seconds he would spit in the ground, his face screwed up in disgust. It was quite apparent he was enjoying this about as much as I was. José repeated this process about ten times until his actions started to tickle.

"Okay, I think you got it all. Good job, José!" Daniel grabbed at his torn shirt and ripped off another piece. José pulled away, and Daniel wrapped a piece of the cloth around my ankle.

I watched as José knelt down by the stream, cupping a hand full of water into his mouth, then spitting it back out. My feelings for him changed that day.

José just saved my life.

Chapter Thirteen

Medicine

"We need to stay here for the night," Daniel stated. "I'll go gather up some wood."

"José? Thank you." I mumbled. My hands were shaking. I tried to stand, but my legs were too wobbly.

"No worries, Shelby, you'd do the same for me, friend." I could hear the grin in his voice.

The next morning, I was the first one awake. My leg was stiff and just a little bit sore. I could walk on it, at least. I went to the stream and scooped out some water and splashed it onto my face. The cold dampness refreshed me, and I cupped my hands, drinking it in delicately like a Doe. Daniel silently walked up behind me.

"How do you feel?"

"A lot better, thanks," I replied, turning to him and smiling.

"I guess I'll go scrounge around for something to eat before we move on. It looks like we'll be walking during the day again. Unless you want to rest up here today?" Daniel's voice vibrated off my skin, causing the little hairs on my arms and the nape of my neck to stand at attention.

"No, it's okay... I'm good. We can walk until it gets too hot at least." My voice sounded raspy to my ears.

Daniel kneeled down at my feet. "Can I look at your leg?"

"Sure," I blushed.

I sat down on one of the boulders as he unwrapped the home-made bandage from around my ankle. The cut was red, but not swollen or discolored.

He grinned, "I don't think the snake was poisonous, Shelby. Usually, if it's a poisonous one, your leg will swell and turn colors."

"Really? Cool!" I grinned back in a 'Go-Team' kinda way.

"I'd keep it wrapped up, though. If for no other reason than to keep the dust out of the cut...at least through-out today." Daniel re-affixed my bandage and stood up.

"Thanks, Daniel. For everything." I smiled at him, hoping that didn't come out sounding too overly come-on'ish and knew I failed, anyway.

After Daniel had disappeared, I decided to wake up the lazy bones. Maybe he could help me catch some minnows to eat. I walked over to where he was laying and nudged him with my toe. He moaned and rolled over. I nudged him again.

"Hey, sleepy head, get up!"

"Ugh..."

"Come on, José, we need to get a move on. Get up!" I nudged him a little harder this time.

José moaned and rolled back over toward me. I bent down and tapped him on the cheek lightly. He was hot; more than hot. It was like putting my hand on a small furnace.

"Daniel?" I called out. I look in the direction he had taken.

I bent down onto my knees and pushed José back and forth, "José, please wake up...José?"

He mumbled, "Let'me alone, Shelby...I'm tired."

"José, please get up!" I started to cry a little. This was not good. I jumped up and grabbed an empty water bottle and ran down to the stream scooped it in and ran back then poured it on his face. He jerked and opened up his eyes.

90

"Hey!" he croaked weakly, "What are you doing, Shelby?"

"José, you need to get up!" I stated worriedly.

I hollered again for Daniel. Where did he run off to?

"Can you get up?"

"Shelby, I don't feel so good." José tried to sit up, but failed miserably.

"I think you're sick. Did you drink some of that snake poison?" I asked, thinking he might have swallowed it, and that's what was making him ill. I didn't know the first thing about snakes. Maybe Daniel knew something, but he assured me yesterday it wasn't one of the poisonous kinds.

"I don't think so. I made sure I spit." He put his hands up and covered his ears. "Arg... my head hurts so bad!"

"Hey, what's going on?" Daniel asked from behind me, walking into the clearing.

I was so relieved to see him I almost kissed his feet. "José is sick. I think he might have swallowed some snake poison. He's really hot, and I don't know what to do!" My gut tightened. All I could think about was what if he dies out here with just us?

"First things first. We need to try and get him cooled down." Daniel rushed over and picked him up. He carried him over to the stream and laid him down in it.

On his knees in the water Daniel demanded, "José, open your mouth."

I frowned. What in the world? What could possibly be in José's mouth? I saw him rinse it out myself.

Daniel held José's mouth open. Using one finger, he poked around inside. I watched as Daniel frowned and shook his head. He looked back at me worriedly.

"José is poisoned alright, but not from just snake-juice... he has an abscessed tooth."

"Oh, is *that* all!" I grinned, not getting it. The relief I felt was instant, and I let out a breath that I'd been holding.

Daniel's frown deepened as he shook his head. "You're not understanding me, Shelby... that's *not* good. The snake apparently was indeed of a poisonous variety and the venom got inside his abscess. It just kicked up into high gear."

My relief burst like a bubble. "Oh no, what can we do? Will he die?" Then as an accusation, "I thought you said it wasn't poisonous, Daniel."

"It's not, unless you have something like an abscess exposed to it. Darn it! I should have known."

"How could you have?"

"He confided in me yesterday that his tooth was hurting him. He thought maybe it was his punishment for stealing a candy bar," Daniel said a little sadly.

"Why didn't he say anything to me?" I asked, hurt. I thought I was his best friend. I shook off the question when I saw Daniel's mouth open to answer. It didn't matter right now.

"What are we going to do? I don't know anything about sickness. My mom always gave me pills."

"Daniel didn't hesitate. "Go get me some burned charcoal pieces out of the fire...hurry."

I shook my head, puzzled. "Why?" I couldn't figure out what in the blazes he needed burned wood for.

"Just do it and hurry! I have an idea."

I went to the spot where José had built the fire last night and dug around for some pieces of burned wood. I brought them back over to Daniel. He took them from me and smashed them up in his hand, then added some water and mixed it into a soupy mess.

He propped José up a little. "Open your mouth, buddy."

José's mouth fell open, and Daniel shoved the stuff inside. He moved his fingers around inside his mouth, rubbing vigorously back and forth on his gums. José gagged and almost bit Daniels finger off.

"That stuff is awful!" José garbled weakly.

"It'll soak up that abscess and poison, my friend." He turned to me, "Shelby; we need to get to the closest town. I know we agreed that we would never treck through a big city, but we're going to need to go through Denver. We need to get him some medicine."

"But how? We don't have any money."

"They have free clinics in bigger cites. We'll find one. Trust me, okay?"

I bit my lower lip anxiously. "How are we going to take him? He can't walk that far, being sick and all."

Daniel sighed. "You're right. You stay here with him, and I'll go. I'll move faster by myself. You'll be okay by yourself with him."

No, I wouldn't, my head argued, then out loud, "Yes, of course, I will," I lied. I wasn't going to admit to him I was scared. What if José were to die on me, and me with no shovel to bury him with? I shivered. He's not going to die. I was talking myself into the crazies. No problem, I can do this.

Daniel pulled José half in and half out of the stream.

He laid his hand on my shoulder. "Listen, I'll hurry. Just try to keep the cold water on him. He'll be fine, Shelby."

"You promise?" I asked him. I needed some reassurance that everything was going to be okay. I felt if Daniel said it was going to be okay; then it would be.

"Yes... I promise, cross my heart." He drew an imaginary X across his breast.

I forced a smile and nodded my head.

I used one of my t-shirts and soaked it with the cold water. I dribbled it over José's forehead, watching as it trickled over the sides of his face. I placed the shirt on his head until it heated, then repeated the process all over again. I kept his feet in the water. Daniel said heat originated at the feet. Ha... like I believed that one. It seemed my feet were always cold.

He was so tiny lying there. The sun was beating down on my head, so I decided it was my turn to get cool. I waded out and squatted just enough to get wet, and then went back to José. My stomach rumbled out a warning that it was time to find something to eat. I scrounged around in José's backpack looking for a half-eaten candy bar or one of the bags of nuts we had picked up but came up empty. Taking out his little hook and spring, I tied it to a limb like he taught me to and went scrounging for some bait. I dug some holes near the marshy area of the pond and found some small worms, carefully hooking a few on a small hook and tossed it in. There was a time not too long ago when even the idea of skewering a squirmy worm to a hooked needle would have turned me green, but not anymore.

I waited patiently, keeping one eye on the pole for any signs of twitches and the other on José, who seemed to be sleeping now. It wasn't long before I had caught a small catfish, then another. I ran back and forth from the pole to soaking José with the cold water, making sure to dribble some of the water in his mouth, as well.

I had to build a fire to cook the little buggers. I watched José do it a million times, so figured how hard could it be? I gathered the limbs and placed them in the same spot as he did last evening then picked up two sticks and rubbed them together like I saw he had done. It didn't work. I tried again. Still didn't work. I couldn't for the life of me figure out what I was doing wrong. I went in search of more sticks, trying those instead, thinking maybe I had picked 'faulty' sticks the first time or something. It still didn't work. I stopped my foot in frustration.

"Shelby?" José groaned.

I ran over to him grabbing the shirt from off his forehead and soaked it again.

"I'm right here, José."

"I'm sorry to be such a pain in your butt."

"You're not," I said, my heart all but breaking. "Are you hungry? I caught some fish," I stated impishly.

He tried to grin, "Nah, but thanks anyway. Maybe later."

"Okay. Hey, José? How did you get the fire to work?" I asked sheepishly.

"With my lighter," he said quietly.

"Oh." I felt chagrined. Now I remembered... he didn't rub the sticks together, he used them to light the rest of the wood. I was only paying half-attention so forgot this rather important piece of information.

"Where is it?"

"In my pocket."

"Hmmm," I frowned. His pants were totally soaked by now. I got up and wandered back to the sticks. I heard that sushi was good.

Thankfully, I didn't get to try any of that delicacy. After many attempts, the sticks finally started to smoke, and then as I had piled dry leaves around like a little teepee, it finally caught. I built the fire up and after cleaning them, (another José lesson I learned) I stabbed both fish with skinny branches and placed them over the makeshift grill José had set up. After they had been thourely cooked, I offered some to José but he wouldn't eat. I ate a few bites, feeling guilty the whole time. All I could think about was José stealing that candy bar because he had been hungry.

José was sick through the night and all the next day. He still wouldn't eat. I helped him up once to do his business. I dug a hole and splayed two limbs across as a potty for him to use. I left him by the tree to allow his privacy, counting the seconds before I might have to check on him to make sure he was okay and hopefully not catch him doing, 'Number Two', thus embarrassing him. He saved me from this though by calling out to me when he was finished.

He never asked me to help him after that; he just wet his pants. I could smell it and knew how embarrassing it felt by my own, personal experience. I knew it had nothing to do with his pride... he was simply too weak to make the trip, which told me that if Daniel didn't come back, and soon... it may be too late.

I drug him back and forth in and out of the creek-bed and let him lie there for a while to both refresh and clean him up a little. He didn't mind and sighed contently every time I placed him in the cool water. If José had been any bigger, there would have been no way I could have done this. This was one of the times I was thankful he was so small. Sometimes I would still forget he was older than me, but now that didn't factor in, whatsoever. He was more like a brother than an age.

Daniel made it back on the third day with loaded with medicine. He had both liquid and pills and gave both to José. When I asked how he got them, he just smiled and said, "Remember my trick?"

I nodded saying nothing. My only thought was; I'm falling in love with him.

Chapter Fourteen

Train Ride

We stayed at our camp for three more days while José slowly recuperated. It didn't take long before he was back up on his feet, (wobbly as his legs were) and making his own bathroom visits. It seemed to me he made these trips about every ten minutes and when I voiced my concerns to Daniel about this, he just smiled and assured me that it was only a side effect of the antibiotics and would pass. It was a good thing, too... the leaves we had to use seemed to be dwindling in supply faster than they could fall.

It was after this period when José got strong enough to continue that we left. We traveled at a faster speed because of the days we had lost. I glanced over at my boys, *my boys*... in a different light. We were a team, no doubt about that fact, now more than ever. For the first time in my young life, I felt like I had a true family. These boys were my family and of course, Oreo, our little egg provider. We got back to our routine of traveling at night and resting in the day and still kept close to the highways and interstates, unless we had to bypass a big city. Then we kept to country roads.

One evening I could have sworn on the Holy bible I saw the familiar maroon Chrysler pulled over at a rest stop. We usually stopped and washed up at these rest areas, but not this one. I told the boys it wasn't a good idea, and we kept to the tree line behind the brick building. José didn't think it could possibly be the same one, but I knew better. I remembered that scratch on the left side.

It was hot. Sweat was pouring a steady stream down my face and into my eyes. Even my palms were wet. I was burning up, having trouble breathing. The air was thick inside the car. All the windows were rolled up tight. The doors were locked, and I screamed...

"Shelby, are you okay?" Daniel asked.

I shook myself. I looked at them both noticing the worry on their faces.

"Yeah, I'm fine. I was just remembering when I had put that scratch on the door." The punishment for that was one I will never forget.

****

One late afternoon we had stopped in a small farming town. A large cart full of fruit and vegetables being towed by a lady was parked alongside the road. She had on a large, straw hat cocked to the side on her head, and was sitting on the back of the truck's tailgate. Daniel walked up and asked her if she had any bruised ones that she might be kind enough to give us. She nodded and said as a matter of fact, she did indeed have a few. She put some in a bag and handed them to him. We thanked her, and after we had got down the road a ways, we opened and looked inside.

Daniel pulled out three large peaches. He handed one to José and myself and took the last for himself. I didn't see any bruises anywhere on the fruit. I asked José if he had any on his, to which he held it up, inspecting it with a half-interested eye, (he already having eaten about half of it) and proclaimed through a full mouth he didn't see any either. I smiled at Daniel who smiled back in a, *See? There are still some good people in the world!* kind of way.

We walked along the railroad tracks singing bawdy songs, making up the lyric as we went.

"Old Jack Horner, sat in a corner, eating his corn and dogs, when up came a spider, and bit him on the finger..."

We were off-key and terrible, but we didn't mind. The worse the lyrics were, the harder we laughed. The sun was beginning to go down when I heard the whistle of the sound of a train.

We all three got this kind of excited look in our eyes. I guess we were all thinking the same thing. We were going to jump a train.

Daniel grinned down at José, "Are you up for a new adventure?"

José laughed, "As long as it's a good one."

I knew I could run fast and jump high, but how was José ever going to make it?

Daniel handed Oreo over to me. "Put him in your pack, Shelby."

I nodded. I watched Daniel pick up José and swing him onto his back. "Hold on, buddy. Don't let go unless you want to meet up with us in a month or so."

José scoffed and bopped Daniel on the head, knowing he was kidding. They were the Three Musketeers plus one bird, after all.

I tucked Oreo inside my backpack.

"Get ready!" Daniel yelled. The train was getting closer. We could see it now as it came around the bend behind us. We stepped back. The wheels hissed and squeaked as the train braked slowly, then stopped.

I looked at Daniel and caught his eye. He frowned. He was probably wondering the same thing as I was...why did it stop? There wasn't anything here. We watched as some men got out and opened up one of the boxcars. I laughed when I saw cows were being led down the ramps out into the field beyond. They must belong to some farmer.

This was perfect. Now we had an empty car to travel in. When the men were preoccupied, Daniel, José, (who was still attached to his back) and I snuck in and crept to the back far corner where it was dark and there were some wooden pallets to hide behind in case one of train guys decided to look in.

"We did it!" José squealed

"Yes, we did!" Daniel patted him on the back.

I took off my pack and reached for Oreo. I was sure he would love this place. There certainly was enough cow-poop in here, which meant bugs, and for him that translated to a feast.

We quieted as the sound of muffled voices came closer followed by the sound of the doors being slid closed, shrouding us in darkness. I heard the sound of a whistle blow again, and the train slowly began rolling out.

I closed my eyes, letting the motion of the ride rock me to sleep. We rode the train until the next stop. Daniel said we couldn't ride on the train too far, as more than likely they would be picking up another load of cows or something and thus blowing our cover. I agreed, so when we stopped we jumped out, but not before it took all three of us to get the boxcar doors open. Once we did, at first panicking a little that they might be locked from the outside, (thankfully they weren't...just rusty) we quickly jumped and ran.

We landed in another small town. We had to ask a man on the street where we were.

"Mississippi," he stated with his Southern drawl.

Wow, it sure didn't feel like we had traveled six-hundred miles on the train. Daniel figured it was probably just being in almost total darkness that messed with our inner clocks. We made up for our lost days and then some. I looked over the map. The town we were in was about the same as the last, being it was small with old wooden buildings adorning the main street. It looked like an old western town, and if a carriage pulled by horses happened by, I probably wouldn't have blinked an eye. We kept to the back roads and walked along a creek bed, traveling southeast.

We were getting close, and my stomach was tying up in knots now.

Chapter Fifteen

Moonshine

"Look." José pointed to what looked like a silver set of jugs on sticks.

Daniel held José back. "Don't go over there, José. That's stuff for grownups."

"What is it?" José as always was too curious to stay away. He ducked under Daniel's arm and ran over to the stands.

I walked at a slower pace. I really didn't care what it was, but the closer I got, the cooler it looked. A large metal jug sat on one end, and a copper tube ran around it like a crazy straw, ending up in another jug.

"Moonshine!" José exclaimed. "This here is moonshine. It's what the back-wood folks call Devil-Juice. They make this stuff and then sell it."

Daniel almost slapped José's hand when he tentatively reached out. "Don't mess with it. The guys who made this stuff will be back to get it, and I don't think we need to be here when they do." Daniel backed up and glanced around wearily.

"I've never tried it before. I want to. Who's with me?" José asked, looking right at me.

I have never consumed a lick of alcohol before in my life. I saw what it did to Jack and wanted no part of that. "I don't think so, José."

"Oh, come on ya big babies, just a taste. I dare you!"

He dared me. Well, darn it to hades. I can't back out of a dare.

I glared at him. "One sip, that's all!"

"Shelby, don't listen to him," Daniel pleaded.

I grinned over at him, "Sorry Danny boy, but a dare is...well, a challenge. Once a dare is made, I can't chicken out." I glanced at Oreo, "No offense."

José found a small tin cup sitting on a stump next to the fifty-two gallon jugs. He pulled off the copper hose and held it over the cup. What followed was a steady, drip, drip, drip.

"Is that all? That'll take forever to fill up. No wonder they left it out here!" I muttered.

José sat the cup down. "Hold this," he said. During all this, Daniel just stood back, shaking his head.

I held the copper tube, while he tried to lift the jug. It was too heavy for him, so we switched places. I lifted the jug and poured a cup. It was clear like water, but the smell cleared the sinuses and burned my eyes.

"Okay, you first," José said handing the cup to me.

"Oh no, you don't, you go first. You made the challenge!"

"Fine," He grumped. He held his nose and drank half the cup and sat it down. I held back laughter as his face first turned beat-red, then he began coughing and gagging, jumping up and down like a rabbit with its tail on fire.

I looked at Daniel. He was looking at José with a smirk on his face. After a few minutes, José picked up the cup and handed it to me. He smiled evilly.

"Your turn." I noticed his eyes were now bloodshot, and I could have sworn he had said, "Your shurn."

I quickly tried to think of a way to get out of this, but I knew José would never let me live it down if I didn't at least try it. I looked down at the clear liquid. How bad could it be, anyway? I plugged my nose and closed my eyes and swallowed. Instant fire burned my throat all the way to my belly. My eyes watered, I guess to put out the fire in my belly. It didn't help. I covered my hand over my mouth so I wouldn't throw up. I kept swallowing even after my mouth dried up, hoping to put out the fire and keep the bile down. With tears running down my face, I looked at José. He was laughing at me. I was afraid to look at Daniel in case he was laughing too.

It wasn't long before the fire subsided in my belly and turned into something warm and fuzzy. I grinned.

"Huh, that wasn't sho bad." I giggled. "Daniel, itsh your shurn again." If we had any common sense, we might have stopped right then, but no, that wasn't the case because we didn't have any common sense; at least José nor I had any. Daniel, on the other hand, had plenty.

"I think I'll pass." he replied as if bored.

"Oh, you big baby." I said and giggled again. I felt wonderful. I felt almost light, as if I could fly. Well, not that light, but almost. I took his hand. "Come on, jush one ship!" I pleaded. He shook his head and smiled at me.

He is so cute, I thought.

"We need to get out of here before the guy who owns this comes back." He turned his eyes on José, "Let's go... now."

"Shhhh!" José held a finger to his lips.

I stopped moving and listened. I could hear twigs breaking under foot and whispers carrying on the breeze. I froze. Daniel motioned us to follow him. We walked quietly but as fast and as far as we could without making a sound. When we reached a good distance away from the moonshine still, we ran as if our pants had caught fire.

The following day, I had a headache that sang to me in bursting colors and on what had to be volume eleven in Dolby stereo surround sound. It pounded right along with my heart-beat, pulsing with every pump. For fun, my stomach joined in, and it didn't take me long to find a quiet place to almost barf out my shoes. At least I wasn't alone... José was only about ten feet from me, crouched and holding his head moaning, "Never again sweet Jesus...just make it go away. I swear to you never, ever again."

I knew the feeling.

David had scrounged up some food for us to eat. Oreo hadn't laid any eggs for the last 2 days. She was probably stressed out from all the action we've been getting lately. Or, I figured, it could have been the cow poop she ate on that train. I was kind of relieved. I was getting tired of eggs. Daniel had gone into town and came back with some biscuits and honey and by now, I had given up on asking him how he got things. I never got a straight answer, anyway.

We sat alongside the same creek bed we had been following since yesterday and ate our biscuits. Daniel sat next to me, his shoulder pressed against my own, making me warm and fuzzy inside despite the headache this was still admonishing me.

"You okay?" he asked.

The biscuit stuck in my throat. "Yep," I mumbled.

"Shelby?" After a long pause, he asked, "How did you end up here?"

I gulped as my heartbeat sped up. I knew what he was asking me, and it was not how did I end up *here*, but how did I end up running. I always knew the question would come up eventually, but I still dreaded having to answer it. I let out the breath I was holding and glanced nervously at José, who was scooting closer as well. He wanted to hear my tale, as well. I picked up a pile of dirt and let it run through my fingers. I watched as the tiny pebbles hit the ground and took my mind back to that place.

"I lived with Mamie and Jack, who was her husband, but not my real daddy. I also thought that she was my real mother but..." I looked up and smiled at them, "she wasn't. Mamie got real sick, and then she died. I found this letter she wrote me the very night she passed away in the hospital."

I took the wadded up paper and handed it to Daniel. I watched his face as he read it. He then passed it to José.

José asked me the dreaded question. "Were they mean to you, then?"

I looked down unable to meet their eyes and possibly see the pity in them. "Why are you asking me that?"

"You talk in your sleep, Shelby," José whispered.

"No," Daniel interjected, "You scream in your sleep, sweetie."

My face burned, but there was nothing I could say to that. I couldn't keep my walls up when I was defenseless and sleeping, after all. I supposed a girl can't keep her secrets forever.

"I guess they were sometimes mean... but Jack was, I mean he was..."

I clamped down on that and shut down. I didn't want to talk about this. Not now and not ever! I stood up. "José, what's your story?"

José shrugged and glanced at Daniel, who nodded to go ahead. They both sensed that I gave them everything I was willing to share at that point, and let's drop the subject, thank-you-very-much.

"My parents didn't want me, so they gave me up for adoption. I heard they were drug addicts, and they sold me for drugs." he shrugged. "I was bounced around from one foster family to another but I knew none of them wanted me, so I left."

"Well," I said. "We're your family now. Aren't we, Daniel?" Daniel smiled, but the smile didn't quite reach his eyes. I frowned, wondering exactly what *his* story was.

Chapter Sixteen

The Cabin

Summer was leaving us behind, and fall was fast approaching. The leaves were turning pretty shades of oranges and browns, and the air held a crisp bite to it. It was time to get rid of the shorts and acquire some long jeans, sweaters and a jacket. When I suggested this to José, he agreed. We found another Goodwill store and picked up some winter clothes, which we traded for our summer ones. Not a good trade in my opinion as we left with less than we came in with and honestly, think they just felt sorry for us and accepted the trade. I picked out two new pairs of jeans and a nice warm jacket, foregoing the sweater as the lady just shook her head at me when I brought them up.

"You have to give up something, honey," she informed me in a dour voice.

Daniel and José did the same. We found a church that served hot food, and they even packed us a lunch to take with us so for the moment at least, we were warm and fed.

We had just left another small town in Mississippi and were following a river when thunder boomed overhead, and a lightning bolt snapped right ahead of us. I didn't mind the thunder so much, but I hated the lightening. Soon after the downpour began, I was running with Oreo tucked into my bag toward an old hunting cabin we had spotted and were relieved it was both vacant and unlocked. I opened the door, it groaning open with some resistance.

Inside was bare except for an old wooden table and one, three-legged stool. Against the far wall sat a single box spring that I assumed was used for a bed. We all piled up on the springs and lay shivering from the cold and dampness that settled into our bodies from our wet clothes. We stayed inside throughout the storm with the constant lightning flashes across the sky, being our only lighting in the dark cabin.

José went snooping in the cupboards and found us a few cans of chili and a small pot and pan.

Now we could boil water for Oreo's eggs. No more fried eggs! Yippy! The next day we built a fire and José warmed up the cans of chili in our new pan. I didn't think the chili smelled too good, so I declined. Daniel warned José not to eat it. Later that evening José got sick, throwing up everything his stomach had to give while he was gripped in cramps. Daniel reminded him that he had been warned, which earned him nothing more than the old hairy eye from José. We decided to stay another night in the cabin, but instead ended up staying for three.

The reason was the storm lasted for all of those three days. We stayed inside, only venturing out when there was a brief break in the clouds. It usually only gave us enough time to gather something to eat and some more wood which we would drag in and set like tiddly-winks in the corner to dry out. We told jokes or sang songs. Daniel showed us how to play a game of marbles using rocks.

There were days I often wondered about Daniel. He never talked about himself. When I tried to bring it up, he always changed the subject. He never got dirty, he never got sick, (I myself along with José had come down with a cold about three times now) and I don't even think he sweated like José or I. He hardly ever raised his voice, certainly not like me, anyway. He was kind, smart, patient and seemed to know something about everything. He knew which plants were good to eat; he knew what berries to eat and what berries not to eat, he had this second-sense of trouble around the corner and always just gently steered us away until he felt it was 'safe'. When José had been sick, Daniel had carried him on his back for miles. He never complained. If the sun hit him just right, I swear I could see a halo. I wanted to know who or what he really was and more importantly...why was he here?

"It's okay if you like him," José stated out of the blue on our last day at the cabin. He sat down beside me.

I pretended I didn't know what he is talking about. "I like you both, José."

"I meant it's okay if you like him more than just a friend." He eyed me with a bit of humor in his eye. "Yea, I know... I can read you like a book by now, Shelb's." He had picked up his new nick-name for me a few weeks ago and seemed to have fallen in love with it. I didn't mind.

I smiled. I did like him more than just a friend, but I won't admit it; at least not to José and *definitely* not to Daniel.

"Thank you for giving me your permission, José... but I like you both as just brothers, okay?" I wrapped my arm around him.

José smiled at me, not fooled in the least.

Chapter Seventeen
The Birthday Wish

Time seemed to fly out here. Days ran into weeks that ran into months and the next think I knew, it was my birthday. I would never have known if José hadn't found an old newspaper someone had discarded. We were in a camping park and had just got done swimming and goofing off. José dug around inside a garbage can-- looking for Only God knows what, nothing I was going to eat that's for sure--when he found the wadded up paper. He opened it to see what was going on in the world when I saw the date stamp was September 4th, my birthday.

"How could I have forgotten my own birthday?" I said under my breath. Of course, Daniel overheard me.

"It's your birthday, Shelby?"

"Yeah, September 4th," I mumbled. Some birthday this was, I thought. However, it ended up becoming the best birthday I had ever had. I forgot for a moment that it probably wasn't my real one but it was the only one I knew.

Once Daniel found out it was my birthday, he went off to do some searching. At least that's what he said. What he actually did was speak to some nearby campers and between all of them, José and Daniel had put together a little party with balloons, brownies, instead of cake topped with candles. They all sang happy birthday, and we were invited to a wiener roast afterward.

Later, I thought it odd that not one person had asked where are families were at. I knew this wasn't the way most grown-ups acted. Here we were, three kids in a campground with backpacks on our backs and no grown-ups with us. What does that tell someone? Usually, this revelation would send the average adult into a game of twenty-questions, one fired after the other. I realized at those points I didn't ever what to be a grown-up if it meant harassing kids all day long if the opportunity arose. Coupled with that, you could look in their eyes and see they weren't even interested in the answers! They were an uncaring lot. When I asked Daniel about it, he said it's not that they didn't care, it's that they were too busy with their own life's problems and generally asked as it was what he called, 'conditioned response', whatever the heck *that* was.

I guess in a way I was glad they were too busy to notice, but on the other hand it made me angry. Maybe, if someone had cared just a little about me, I would have been found before Jack showed up.

The few kids that I did see with their parents seemed to be happy enough. They laughed and played and to my amazement, when I looked for marks or bruises on them, I didn't see any.

Chapter Eighteen
Deer

Daniel swung his arm out to stop us.

"Look."

My eyes follow the direction to where he is pointing. Three deer stood to the right of us along the other side of the road. "It's a doe and her babies."

I stopped and watched as they ate and played. They darted across the road just as a truck veered around the corner from out of nowhere, barreling right toward them. I screamed and waved my arms, but it was too late. The momma deer ran and got away with one baby, but the other lay broken in the road. The truck swerved, slowed then sped away again.

I ran over to where the fawn lay. He or she was still alive. He bleeped, and a tear ran down his face.

"Daniel, we have to help him. Do something, *please*." I was begging and crying at the same time.

"Move out of the way." Daniel picked up the fawn and carried it over to where José stood.

"Come on, let's find a spot to lay him down and see if we can find out what's wrong with him."

"It's a he?" I asked, following him. Daniel didn't answer but silently kept walking. I follow them as they trampled through the weeds, looking for a good spot.

José stopped and bent down. "This will do." He brushed twigs aside and pulled some grass to make a soft bed. Daniel lay the fawn down his hands rubbing over the gentle creature's legs and back.

The fawn gasped, then lay limply. It was the saddest thing I have ever seen in my entire young life. I didn't know if I could keep myself from crying, but I sure tried. My eyes burned and the back of my throat itched.

"He's gone." Daniel sat back on his heels. He looked at me with sorrow-filled eyes. That made me want to cry even more.

José stood up and brushed the dirt off on his pant legs. "Well, looks like we're going to have deer steak for dinner tonight."

I gasped and looked up at him in horror. "Are you crazy? I'm not eating Bambi!"

José laughed and slapped his thigh. "You're so funny, Shelbs. That's not Bambi. If we don't eat him, something else will. He's already dead."

My eyes swung back to Daniel pleading for help but found none. He stood up and turned to me but didn't meet my eyes. "He's right Shelby...its food and he's already dead."

The coward couldn't even look at me when he said it. I couldn't believe these two. With my hands on my hip, I yelled at the top of my lungs, "*I'm* not *going to eat him!*"

"Suit yourself," José said nonchalantly, unimpressed with my outburst and grabbed a long stick. "Come on Daniel, let's build a fire and get to cutting before the blood settles."

I ran for the bushes and threw up everything that was in my stomach, which wasn't much to begin with.

Unwilling to go back to camp to watch the procedure of whacking up the baby deer, I followed a trail that lead to a rocky cliff, , reverently soaking in the beautiful horizon that was before me. I stood upon a large boulder high above the rock-strewn river that was rushing, spewing a mist to chill the morning air. All the golden colors of fall sure made everything more beautiful in their untainted state as of yet untouched by mans progress in this part of

112

the woods. I could see José and Daniel from where I stood, cooking.

"Are you all right?" Daniel asked me a couple hours later as I sat on a rock, my back to the river.

"No, I am not all right. How could you do it?"

"Shelby, deer were put on this earth to serve. There's nothing wrong with eating it. Remember, we didn't kill it to begin with...it was already dead." He touched my shoulder gently. "Did it ever cross your mind that it was killed so we could have food? There is a reason for everything that happens."

I look at him with moisture pooling in my eyes. "There's a reason for everything that happens, huh? So answer me this, why was I kidnaped when I was a baby, Daniel? Why?" I jumped up and balled up my fists. I stomped off for added effect, wanting him to know that in my opinion it wasn't all right; deer were not just food, little boys didn't have to go through life as a dwarf and babies shouldn't be taken. Daniel watched me huff off, saying nothing. He nodded to himself and was as always, patient.

Late that night my stomach growled uncomfortably. By now I am so hungry I felt like I could eat a whole cow and wished I had eaten some of the doe, after all. I kept silent, though... resolved in my stubbornness as there was no way I would let them know I was a traitor to my own cause.

On his side and rolled up in a thin blanket but not asleep, Daniel lay and listened to her tummy grump and growl, admiring her strong will to stick to what she felt was right.

Chapter Nineteen

Alabama

Welcome to Alabama, the beautiful

The green signpost read the greeting with its signature eagle logo proudly. Beautiful what? I wondered as I marched past it. The boys dragged behind. Daniel was carrying Oreo, and I picked up my pace, excitement filling my belly. According to the map, we were almost there.

Home.

Did I call it that?

Is it my home?

What if they're not there anymore? What if they moved? I passed each thought, quickly moving to the next like my brain was shuffling cards instead of thoughts.

Will they want me now that I'm grown?

What if they find out that I've been bad and ran away...would they still want me?

I coughed. I had a tickle in my throat that wouldn't go away.

Perfect, I thought. *Just what I need right now...a cold.*

"Shelbs, wait up," José grunted from behind me.

I slowed down and slid off my jacket. One thing was for sure; it was hot in Alabama. The trees were still green and full giving the impression summer was still in full swing, despite the fact it was late October. We passed fall awhile back and up until now; all the trees had been an array of autumn colors; browns and oranges, mixed in with yellow and crunchy brown to step on. However, not here; ere the trees were as green as August...even the grass.

Daniel caught up to me and bumped my arm, looking at me. "Your face is red."

"It's awfully hot," I commented, noting the bright sky and the warm breeze that had just picked up.

Daniel looked over the hill that was covered in wild flowers and remarked on what I was just reflecting on not a moment ago. "It doesn't feel like fall, does it?"

I coughed. "Sure doesn't."

José caught up with us. "I love it, Shelbs. It's summer *and* winter. It's awesome! I hate snow. I could get use to this."

"Yeah, me too," I mumbled. "I need something to drink, guys. My throat is parched."

"It's not much further to the town of Athens," Daniel said. "I vote we hitch a ride."

Daniel knew how I felt about hitch-hiking a ride from a stranger. Who knows what creeper may be behind the wheel, maybe just waiting for the chance to pick up three teens (one of them a pretty, young teenage girl, at that!) and do God only knew what with them. More importantly, what if it ends up being Jack who stops? He might have bought a new vehicle by now.

"How much farther to Athens?" I asked.

Daniel pulled the map out of his back pocket. He frowned then looked back at me.

"Fifteen miles...give or take."

I groaned loud enough for them both to hear. With the way, I felt right then I knew that was too far for me to walk, and I knew it. I was about dying of thirst and for a moment our canteens were completely dry.

I nodded my head, "Okay, then we hitch."

Daniel took my hand gently, "Shelby; it'll be alight. I won't let him get you." His words made my heart both soar and feel a stab of pain. What could this sweet, intelligent man-boy do against the likes of Jack? Jack would eat him up first before spitting him back on the ground. Daniel didn't let go of my hand, but gave me a reassuring wink as if he had read my mind and said back, *You have no idea what I'm capable of doing to protect you, Shelby.*

We did have to walk about another two miles before someone picked us up. It was a man and his son; farmers they said. They didn't even blink an eye at Oreo like most folks tended to do. Apparently, seeing chickens was something they were accustomed to. The man let us ride in the back of his truck that was filled with hay bales. That was fine by me. I lifted up my face to the wind. I sneezed the whole way to Athens.

When the man stopped to let us off, he asked in a southern drawl if there was anything else we needed. I asked him where the nearest place for a cold drink of water was. He turned his head and said something to the boy on his right. The next thing I knew, he was holding a bottle of water out toward me.

"Here ya go, ma'am."

I was never so glad to see a bottle of water in my whole life. I thanked him profusely and proceeded to chug the whole bottle of water down. When I looked up, an embarrassed flush swept up my neck. The farmer smiled with a sparkle in his eye.

"I guess you were thirsty," he said, laughing.

"I guess I was," I smiled back shyly. Daniel frowned and looked at me sharply. I instantly felt terrible for not offering them a drink but didn't get it that Daniel was worried about me...not about water. The kind farmer handed each of the boys a bottle, pulling them from the cooler and handed me an extra one with a wink.

"In case that thirst comes back, young lady."

"Thank you," I said in a small voice. He just nodded as all good county-folk did when given a thank you. To them, it was all they needed in their eyes to even the score up.

"You kids take care now," he said before he drove off.

After we had gone through the small town of Athens, we kept close to the highway. The terrain was nothing like Wyoming or Colorado. No mountains for one and the foliage and trees were thick here. I noticed a large cotton-like fabric in a tree and asked Daniel what it was. He said it was a spider's web. That had to be the biggest spider ever to make a web that large. I shivered at the thought. He said we would see a lot of them in the south.

The first time I got a good look at a palm tree, I wanted to hug it just to say that I did. Don't ask me why, but it seemed to scream at me, *Welcome to Florida! Welcome to Paradise!* It was the neatest tree I had ever seen in my book. I've never seen one before. To be honest, they were actually kind of ugly; what with no real leaves but instead just big, hanging palms,

Also no coconuts, I noted dourly.

But still neat. Wyoming didn't have anything like it. Daniel said wait until we see the ocean. He said that was a sight I would never forget. The water is clear, and you can see to the bottom near the shore and all matter of life that swam in it or just lay there. I couldn't imagine clear water. He also said the beaches had sand white as snow.

"Can you fish in it?" asked José, as always the practical one, (usually 'practical' meaning whatever led to his stomach) as he looked at Daniel curiously.

"Oh ya, the fish are huge!" Daniel assured him.

We passed a field full of cotton, which of course I had to investigate, and I now had a wad of cotton in my pocket. We passed a field of peanuts. I couldn't believe it! Peanuts, of all things! I added a pocket of those, too. Daniel told us not to eat them raw. They were disgusting. I believed him without a second thought. I have learned not to second-guess Daniel by now. I could wait. How does he know all this stuff, I wondered? Back home I knew it was probably snowing by now. Even with the Alabama heat pumping down on our heads, I knew it was October because the houses we passed had pumpkins on the porches and scarecrows in the yards. Witches and ghosts hung from trees in festive places, marking the upcoming trick or treat night.

"Does anyone know what day it is?" I asked suddenly.

"Nope," José chimed in.

"Yes, it's October twentieth," Daniel answered.

Of course, he would know. I thought, shaking my head a little. Halloween was just around the corner. I shivered. I got this feeling we were being watched. I scanned the area carefully and glanced at Daniel, catching him doing the same. I saw the worried look on his face right before he covered it up. He feels it too. I wonder if he also heard the car idling in the distance.

Chapter Twenty

The Fever

The next day, we traveled through a large city, but we had no choice this time. We were hungry and thirsty. My clothes were clinging to my sticky skin. The air was thick with moisture and was pressing down on my lungs, making me sound like a wet train going uphill. It's going to rain and hard by the look of the sky, and I was looking forward to that with unrelenting anticipation. Sweat was trickling down my back between my shoulder blades and pooling at the top of my butt now in a steady stream. Daniel grabbed my hand again making me feel warm inside and not just from my fever. He squeezed it gently and led José and myself over to a bench next to the bus stop sign.

"Wait here," he said. He hands me Oreo.

"What? Why? Where are you going?" I asked, trying to keep the edge of panic out of my voice.

"Just wait here a minute. I'll be right back. José keep an eye on her, will ya?"

José and I sat quietly, watching the cars wiz by and the people walking past us.

"I thought you didn't like to be touched," José mumbled a tad stiffly.

"So?" I said.

"Well...you let Daniel hold your hand."

"That's different," I said. I coughed then sneezed. My throat hurts.

"Besides," I said coolly, "I thought you said you didn't mind if I liked Daniel."

"Yea, well, I don't...just don't rub it in, is all." He changed the subject, scooting away from me on the bench. "Sounds like you're getting a cold, Shelb's. Don't give it to me. I'm a big baby when I get sick."

I snorted, "You're already a big baby."

"Har-har," he shot back, making a face at me.

I heard thunder roll in the distance. We looked at each other.

José swung his feet nonchalantly. "It's going to rain."

"Yep." I coughed again. "I wonder where Daniel went off to."

"Probably to get us something to eat. Hey Shelb's, have you noticed how Daniel always finds things and seems to know what's going to happen five seconds before it happens?" He said this off-handedly, but I felt a chill race through me. In a nutshell, José had just summed up Daniel to a tee.

"Yeah, I noticed." I said. Daniel finds things and he seems to know a lot about everything. It was just like this storm coming. I wasn't worried about it, because I know he'll find us shelter; he always found us shelter. Sometimes it seemed like he would miss it by a couple of minutes just for show, even though I was convinced he could have just as easily had them under cover long before the first rain drop hit the ground.. It was like he was our guardian angel. I say us, because it wasn't just me who he watched out for, it was also José.

Oreo was frightened, I could tell. She was hiding her beak in her feathers. I laid my hand on top of her head, cooing. "It's okay, Oreo. We have Daniel." I whispered, feeling both silly and a strange contentment at the same time.

A short while later Daniel comes back, toting a large sack filled with hotdogs, two apiece and three bags of Doritos.

"Did you get us something to drink?" Asked José.

Daniel hands me the bag. "No, they didn't have anything."

"Who?"

"The hotdog vender. But hey, listen...I talked to this kid, and he said there's a church up the road. He said the doors are never locked, and we can hold up there for the night."

José and I look at each other with a knowing grin. He talked to a kid...right. Sure he did.

José jumps up, "Great, let's go!"

"What about Oreo?" I asked.

"No one is around there at night, Shelby. We can take her inside with us."

"Daniel, what if she poops?"

"Well, then José will clean it up" he grinned wickedly.

"Huh? No I won't!" José growled.

Daniel laughed and ruffled his hair. "Don't worry about it, I'll do it."

I coughed in my hand ladylike and 'ewed' to myself at the wad of lung-phlegm it produced.

The exterior lighting of the church was bright enough to blind someone and written with gold over the entrance to the church were the words, *In honorem s. Ludovici. Deo uni et trino dicatum. A. MDCCCXXXIV*. I wondered what that meant and figured it was probably a warning to keep out. The church was a huge cathedral-looking place with a high, vaulted ceiling and large, stained-glass windows in Gothic design. Our voices carried, bouncing off the walls even when we whispered. All the pews were padded. In the front of the room stood an alter with a gold statue of Jesus on the cross. To the left against the wall were small cubicles lined up with only curtains as doors. That must be where people confessed their sins, I thought, not knowing one wit about such things as I was not raised anything really...much less Catholic. I stare at the rooms with envy. Boy, could *I* spend a couple of hours in there! I sat Oreo down on the gray carpeting. She fluffed out her wings and went to pecking at invisible bugs. I coughed again.

More icky stuff...yuck. Now it was hurting even more to cough, each one stabbing my chest like a cold ice-pick and being slower and slower to easing up.

The padded pews look comfortable and inviting enough to sleep on. For reasons I didn't understand, I felt safe here; as if the room itself carried a sense of protection. It was like being enveloped in a warm hug.

"I'm going to see if I can find some water," I said hoarsely. I went back towards the entrance and turned right down the corridor. A sign above a door signified it was a woman's restroom.

I crept in cautiously and saw four stalls lining the back wall. The room held an aroma of roses and cleanliness. I walked straight over to the faucet and turned on the tap to cold, dunking my whole head underneath and open my mouth letting the water flow in. I gasped at first, swearing to myself that I wouldn't have doubted if steam weren't coming up from my burning scalp and face. I felt as if I couldn't get enough. I splashed more water on my face, my skin seeming to drink in the water as much as the mouth was. I looked up and stared at the reflected image, seeing a stranger. My face is almost cadaverous, and dark circles lined my sunken eyes. A second later I rushed to the first stall and emptied my stomach.

When I was down to nothing but dry-heaves, I went back to my sink and rinsed my mouth out, trying to drink some more water. I held a small amount down with the struggle and snatched a mint out of the glass bowl that adorned the porcelain and popped it in my mouth. I leaned my back against the wall and closed my eyes. My throat felt as if I had swallowed a razor blade with every swallow. I wearily pulled away and shuffled back out, sneezing again and now moaned out at the combined pain in my throat and chest.

****

It hurts. The little girl crawls across the room on all fours dragging one leg behind. She leaves a trail of blood. Mommy help, Mommy...

Mommy looks at her, but her eyes are gone. She sees me and doesn't see me. She opens her mouth to tell me everything's going to be okay but instead the little girl sees nothing but a bottomless pit where tongue and teeth should be. Mommy points to a little girl and says through the hole, "Shush baby-dumpling. I'm gone, but there is a protector for you now. A protector...a protector...a...

I opened my eyes to darkness. It takes a minute for my heart to slow. I try to block out those memories, but they often find a way in. It's always in through my dreams. Oh God, I just want to tear out my hair!

I can hear José's heavy breathing. I took a deep breath myself and winced at the wrack of pain it caused. I forced myself to sit up. The room spins and wobbles and I bite back a groan. The room is cast in shadows. I stood up on wobbly legs and made my way slowly down the aisle towards the glow. When I reached the statue of Jesus, I kneeled and bowed my head. I have so much I want to ask Him, but for some reason it won't come out. I stayed silent, letting the tears slide down my cheeks unabashed.

I'm not sure how long I kneeled there, but it was long enough that Oreo came hunting me down. He pecked at my toes. I twisted and picked him up.

"You're supposed to be asleep," I whispered hoarsely in my croaky voice. I stood back up and made it (barely) to the first pew. I laid back down with Oreo tucked under my arm.

I woke myself up once again, this time coughing so wretchedly I woke Daniel up.

"Are you alright?" He asked from out of the darkness.

"Yeah," I rasped. I feel a hand on my forehead.

"Shelby, you're burning up."

"It's just a cold. I'll be okay."

"Hold on, let me get you a cold rag." Daniel disappears, only to reappear a minute later. I feel something cold against my forehead.

"Thanks," I sighed. It felt wonderful.

"I'm going to go see if I can find some aspirin. I'm sure they have some around here."

"Be careful, Daniel. I don't want you to get in trouble," I yawned, oblivious to who in the world he would get in trouble *from*, much less where he would find aspirin.

"Shelby, I don't think anyone would be too upset if I were trying to find some aspirin for a sick girl."

"Okay," I replied before I succumbed to the darkness pulling at my eyelids.

"Shelby, wake up."

I opened my eyes, and Daniel is sitting next to me, holding what looks like a glass of water and two white pills.

"Here, drink this and take these."

After I take the pills and wash them down with the cool water, I went back to sleep, this time dreamless.

Chapter Twenty-One

Evil Follows

Another morning is here, and we're on the tail end of a memorable journey. I wondered how many miles I have put on these legs. At least it's a beautiful day to be walking. The sun is shining, and I can see deer feeding in the fields around me. I just wish I had better shoes because the gravel road we were on was starting to hurt my feet. I still felt weak, but better than the night before. Between the beautiful trees and surrounding corn fields; coupled with the hot Alabama sun and the sounds of nature all around, I felt a bit like I was in a fairytale. Nonetheless, I still had this chill that kept running up my spine and made my stomach churn.

I sniffed like a hunting dog on point. The peaceful surroundings are filled with an ominous feeling of terror and dread and I jumped a little every time we came to a bend in the road or a tree that seemed big enough for somebody to hide behind. My mind started racing, and I started to feel panic set in.

I heard the idle of a vehicle somewhere behind me, but I was too terrified to turn around. I stopped for a second to gather myself and prayed that it was all just in my head. Daniel also stopped. José kept walking, oblivious to what might be going on. I took a deep breath and heard the sound getting closer. Daniel and I started to walk faster, and my heart was pounding so hard it was all I could hear now. Images of me being found mutilated on the side of the road started to run rampant through my head. Even the trees and scarecrows seem to be watching me, and the deer had all vanished from the fields.

I decide to turn around and put a stop to all this nonsense and prove to myself that he's not there. My knees got weak, and I felt my stomach sink just as I saw a shadowy figure coming out from behind a tree. I can't make out what he looked like with the sun shining in my eyes, but something was definitely there, and here we are, stuck in the middle of nowhere. The chance that someone is just out for a stroll in the middle of nowhere between mile marker 116 and 117 was more than unlikely. I pressed on even faster now trying to think what to do, where to go, how to survive one more time in this life that seemed to keep throwing curve balls at me. Will these be the last thoughts I have? What will he do to me if he catches me? My mind is racing. I'm not even sure I can remember to breathe.

Don't look back, just look forward and keep going. Maybe it will go away.

Daniel can see the fear on my face, I'm sure. José is oblivious to what is going on behind him.

"Hey!" A stranger hollers. I stopped cold; frozen to the ground. "You guys haven't come across a German Shepard on your walk, have you?" the man asked cheerfully.

Daniel shook his head, "No sir... no dog, just a bunch of deer."

"Alright, sorry to have bothered you." The man waved offhandedly and turned, disappearing back into the trees.

I stood there panting, my eyes wide with fear and shaking uncontrollably. Daniel looked at me sympathetically. "Shelby, it's okay, he's gone."

My eyes are locked on José. He stopped and turned when the man spoke. He read the fear on my face and knew what I was thinking and shook his head a little sadly. The shock still held me for a moment.

He found me! was my only thought.

126

José looked over at Daniel, "What's going on?"

I jumped when Daniel touched my arm. "Shelby, it's alright, he's gone."

"No, it's not *alright*, Daniel. It was *him*." I knew that voice...it haunted my dreams at night and consumed my days when awake. I now knew he had been following us.

"You mean your step-dad?" José asked, baffled. "That was him? How did he find you?" In the back of his mind, he wondered if that were so, why didn't he just grab her or something?

I nodded my head. "He must have been following us the whole time."

Daniel took my hand again. "That doesn't make any sense. Why didn't he stop you?" he asked, reiterating what José had just thought.

Pressing a hand to my nervous stomach, I replied, "I don't know."

Daniel wrapped his arm around me. "He won't get you; I won't let him, don't worry."

José chimed in, "*We* won't let him get you, Shelb's. He'll have to get through us first."

Why Jack didn't attack or come after me here in the middle of nowhere was a mystery to me. What was he up to? Why didn't he say something to me? My stomach clinched in fear, knowing exactly why. Daniel. If Daniel hadn't been here, he probably would have, but he didn't want witnesses or a fight, no matter how much one-sided it may be. José he could handle with one swipe of his hand, Daniel, not so much. But still, he wanted me to know that he had found me.

"Come on, let's get out of here," José mumbled as his eyes scoped the area.

We all three walked faster. It amazed me how José could walk so fast for one so small. I carried Oreo this time, feeling just a little safer with her in my arms. Every few minutes, I looked back. I knew he was following. I could feel him, the evil of his shadow.

Chapter Twenty-Two
Laurel Hill, Florida

"It's only ten more miles, Daniel; I can make it!" I told him for the umpteenth time. He wanted us to stop and rest until I felt better, knowing that it wouldn't take much of a push to make me relapse into being sick again, but I felt so close that I didn't want to stop. I *did* feel like crap, but I thought not from being sick, just a general tiredness. Also, I was afraid if we stopped Jack would get me when I was right at the finish line, like some evil Jack-in-the-Box popping out from behind a tree or something. I wanted to get there before he stopped me.

My fever was gone, or so I thought. The aspirins I had been taking seemed to be working just fine...at least for the time being, but recently my skin had taken on a sheen of sweat and I was shivering constantly, despite the warm weather. I had put on my jacket earlier although the sun was beating down on us in the mid-afternoon Florida heat. My eyes darted in every direction, and now my ears were ringing. I kept hearing the idle of the engine. I didn't know if it's just me hearing things, or if it was Jack still following. The fear was now there as constant as the chills that ran through me.

An hour later, I pulled off my jacket, suddenly over-heating. I counted in my head my steps to keep myself from collapsing. Each time I took a breath, my lungs gurgled noisily. My ribs hurt, my head was pounding and my vision was pulsing in and out, but I didn't want to stop. I needed to keep going. We're almost there. We passed a few farms with horses drinking out of the trough. More houses came into view. I'm too tired to keep going. All I really wanted is to sleep in a warm bed. I know I had walked farther than the ten miles the sign stated back there.

José is lagging behind, now the Oreo-bearer. He's so afraid he might catch something he had been keeping a vigilant distance of at least ten feet from me at all times.

Daniel came up beside me, obviously not sharing José's concerns. I am so tired and weak by now I just leaned in against his side. My head pounded, and the pain stabbed behind my eyes with every heartbeat.

"Shelby, you're burning up. We need to stop," Daniel said, concern etched in his strong features.

All I could manage was just one word. "No."

"Alright. Just hold on then... it's not much farther." Daniel sighed, resigned for the moment and leaned back against me to support my weight.

The small white church came into view just as we rounded the corner. My breath hitched in my throat on seeing it. It was the same as in my dream!

A small white church sat back off away from the road surrounded by walnut trees. We stopped there, but I could only stare. I had been here before; I could feel it deeper down inside me; stronger than a dream, stronger than any sense of deja vu. This was *real*, no longer a dream. The church was real, after all. The only difference from my dream was the parking lot. It was gravel.

My legs decided to give out on me. I couldn't walk another step. I moaned out thickly. Every breath I took felt like fire. I was too weak to go on.

"Catch her, she's going to fall!" screamed José', hopping from one foot to the other.

Daniel caught me just before I hit the pavement. I heard him whisper in my ear, "Ah, Shelby, you'll be just fine. You made it. You're home now."

José left Oreo outside the church and he followed Daniel who carried me into the church through the front doors, laying me gently down into one of the pews. He signaled for José to watch me, and then he quietly turned away and without an explanation, walked out.

At first, José assumed Daniel was coming right back that he had gone to get help...but as minutes went by turning into hours, he felt the disappointment deep down.

José yelled for help. "Is anyone here? Please help!" He soon heard footsteps fast approaching. José looked toward the sound. From a side door in the back of the sanctuary came a tall, wiry gentleman.

"How may I help you?"

"Please help! It's Shelby; she's real sick. Can you help us, sir?"

The man's eyes found me as I lay helpless on the cushions of the pew. I can barely make out his features. He quickly kneels down beside me, and I felt a cool hand on my forehead.

"She's burning up," the man exclaimed. I can sense the worry in his tone.

"Yes sir, she's been sick for a while. Please, can you help us?"

The man reached into the front of his jacket pocket and pulled out a cell phone. After punching in some numbers, he spoke briskly to José.

"We need to get her to the hospital. It'll be faster if we take my car. What's your name?" the man asked him.

"I'm José, sir and this here is Shelby, my friend. Just please help her."

"Hello José. My name is Pastor David Williams. We'll get her some help, don't worry."

An older man came in through the front doors. He took in a small group. "Pastor, the van is ready."

With gentle hands, I'm being lifted and then carried out to the waiting white van. "We'll meet you at the hospital," Pastor David said to the older gentleman.

"José?" the Pastor asked, "do you want to ride with me to the hospital?"

"Yes!" José scrambled catching up to him as Pastor David made his way to an older model Chevrolet.

The drive to the hospital took all of ten minutes; José too worried to notice any of his surroundings. When the Pastor and José arrived at the emergency room, the man who first brought the van up was standing in front of the reception, signing some papers.

He glanced up at them then his eyes found José.

"They already took her into the back," the man said to him.

Pastor David nodded. "José, come. Let's sit down here and wait."

José followed and sat next to him in a large waiting room. He twisted his hands together and looked down at the floor, his legs swinging back and forth nervously.

"She'll be okay," The Pastor assured José, "don't worry, she's in God's hands now. They have good doctors here."

José didn't answer. He kept his head bowed.

"Is she your sister?" Pastor David asked.

"No sir, Shelby is my best friend, well... besides Daniel."

"How did you get her inside the church?"

José furrowed his brow and looked up. "Daniel carried her in, but then he had to leave."

The Pastor frowned a little. "Who is Daniel?

"He's our friend. He helped Shelby, and I get here."

"Get here?"

132

"Yes, sir. We've come a long way, already. Shelby is looking for her Momma."

"Ahh... I see. Where did you travel from?" The Pastor asked.

"Wyoming, sir."

"You came all the way from Wyoming... how?" he asked, fascinated.

"We mostly walked, but sometimes we got rides. Not often, though. Shelby doesn't trust strangers and..."

José bit down on the rest of that, not wanting to reveal anything about her step-dad in case the nice Pastor decided to *not* be nice and call Jack to come get her, as she was a runaway.

"Once we even rode the train." José finished lamely.

"You said Shelby was looking for her mom. Who is she...do you know her name?"

"Shelby doesn't know. All she knows is what her other mom told her, and what town she had been taken from and your church...well, it was in her dream. She was taken when she was just a baby. Her fake mom told her all of this in a letter right before she died. Shelby came here to find her real mom."

The Pastor raised his eyebrow, trying to absorb this tragic and moving tale. "How old is Shelby?"

José fidgeted in his seat. "She just had her fourteenth birthday."

"Fourteen is awfully young to be out on her own. How old are you, José?"

"Me, sir? I'm sixteen."

Before the Pastor could question him further, the large doors in front of them swung open, and a man in a long, white jacket walked out. He walked right up to the Pastor and held out his hand.

"Pastor David! Did you bring the girl in?"

"Yes, Paul...how is she?"

The doctor looked down at José and spoke matter-of-factly, "A young girl is severely dehydrated, and she has a fever of a hundred and four. We took her blood, so I'm waiting to hear back from the lab on what we're dealing with. I have her hooked up to an IV now to get fluids in her and started a round of antibiotics. I'm waiting on x-rays on her chest, as well."

The doctor looked directly at José. "What happened to her that you know of to let her get to this state of health?"

José looked up at the Pastor, hoping he would answer the doctor for him. He didn't like hospitals.

Pastor David answered the doctor as best he could, considering he really didn't know much. He explained how the two urchins ended up at his church. When he was finished explaining, something clicked; something from his memory. His eyes widened.

"Wait! José, you mentioned that she was looking for her real mom?"

"Yes sir," José nodded.

"Do you know her mother's name? What is Shelby's last name?"

José shook his head and shrugged, not having a clue and knowing even Shelby couldn't have answered that one.

The Pastor looked back at the doctor. "Listen Paul, can you run a DNA test for me?"

"Sure Pastor, I can do that."

"Great, I need to make a phone call. José, I'll be right back. Don't go anywhere."

José watched the Pastor walk away. The doctor looked back down at him. "José, can you tell me anything else that might help in finding out what's wrong with your friend?"

"No, sir, except I got sick a while back before Shelby; a month ago, or maybe two. I got sick after I ate some soup from a can. It kept coming back up after I ate it, but I don't think Shelby ate any of it."

The doctor nodded at him. He smiled down at José and patted him on the head. "We'll take good care of her. Don't worry."

José sat back down and stared at the tiles. He didn't want to cry, but the tears slipped out anyway of their own free will. He couldn't stop them. He wiped at the traitors and sniffed, just knowing they were going to put him back in foster care. He should just leave now while he had a chance, but no, he knew he couldn't just leave Shelby...at least not yet; not until he knew for certain she would be okay. It wasn't fair that Daniel just left like that. What was his problem anyway? The closer they got, the more withdrawn he had become. José decided he didn't like him anymore. He was a strange one, indeed.

José sighed. Who was he kidding? Daniel was like a brother. He wished he were here. He would know what to do.

"José?"

José jumped when he heard his name. He turned around, and the Pastor was holding out a bottle of water. "Here, you better drink this. We don't want you admitted, as well."

"Yes, sir," José answered. He thanked the Pastor and took the water. He chugged it down and before he realized it; the bottle was empty. He had been thirstier than he had thought.

The Pastor smiled. "Here. I also brought you a Danish from the machine. They don't offer much else in those vending contraptions...nothing good, anyway." The Pastor handed José the sweet roll and José tore into it with relish.

"How long have you two been on the lamb?" the Pastor asked, sitting down.

"The lamb?" José repeated, lifting a brow as he took another bite of his Danish.

"Yes, you know... on the run."

"Oh," José said cautiously. Well, he had trusted him this far, and if was going to call the cops, he figured he probably would have done so by now. "I met Shelby at the beginning of summer. So then, I guess."

"You mean the beginning of last summer?" Pastor David asked incredulously.

"Yea...April, I think."

"José, that was like six months ago. You two have been out there for six months?"

José just nodded his head, not seeing himself how that would be such a big deal. He took another bite and just nodded without answering.

"Where are your parents?"

José kept his eyes on the floor as a sense of panic set in. He knew it! The preacher man was going to put him in a home!

Pastor David noticed the panic on José's face and lowered his voice. "José, it's alright. I'm willing to help you and Shelby, but only if you want me to. I'm not going to force you to do anything. You can trust me, okay?"

"They didn't want me!" José blurted out, puffing up his chest. "That's okay, because I didn't need them, anyway. I've been on my own for a long time now. I was tossed around from one foster home to another. I think I've done pretty well on my own."

The pastor looked José in the eye and saw past his dwarfism. Whatever else this boy was, he sensed this was about the bravest young man he had ever met. "Son, you've done really well for yourself. But you don't have to anymore... not if you don't want to."

Chapter Twenty-Three
Discovery

I opened my eyes and squinted up at the light above my head. I would give anything right now for a tall glass of cold water. The room was quiet except for the closing of a door and a quiet cough somewhere far off. I turned my head and looked up at the man in a white coat. A doctor, I presumed.

"Where am I?" I croaked. I cleared my throat and tried again, pushing the question past my dry, scratchy throat.

"Where am I?"

"You're awake! Good! You're in the hospital. You caused quite a stir, young lady, but you're going to be fine. How do you feel?"

"Thirsty," I said. Thirsty was an under-statement. The doctor was completely gray-haired with small, wire-rimmed glasses that perched on the end of his nose.

The doctor poured a glass of water from a pink pitcher that sat on a table and handed me a glass.

I drank it down swiftly, gulping and held it out for more.

"Shelby, slow down...too fast will cause you to throw it all back up," he said wisely.

I handed him back my glass. "Thank you. How did I get here?"

"I believe your friend brought you in here. You were very sick with a fever. That was two days ago."

I smiled impishly, "Yeah, I haven't been feeling too good."

"No, I bet you haven't." He sat down on a stool beside me.

"Shelby, my name is Doctor Paul Morris. I've been the lucky one taking care of you. Do you remember anything at all?"

I nodded my head. "Yes, my friends. Daniel and José brought me here, right?" My head was still a bit fuzzy, but I remembered the church and someone carrying me.

"Well...I don't know about any Daniel, but yes, José has been waiting in the lobby for you. He's anxious to see you. I'll bring him in, but first I would like to ask you a few questions."

I rubbed my hand against the clean sheets, feeling their softness and wondered about Daniel.

...wondering and worrying.

"José tells us that you came here searching for your parents?"

I saw the concerned look on his face and knew José the big mouth had already blabbed most of the story to him, but decided to appease the good doc. After all, he was helping me to get better.

I told him everything... well, almost everything. I did tell him about Jack and my mom and how I was scared that he would find me. The doctor patted my hand and told me not to worry; they would take care of everything. I believed him, although I wasn't sure who *they* were.

"Thank you for telling me, Shelby. I would like to run some more tests on you, but first the young man is out in the hall waiting to see you." The Doctor stood and walked to the door. When he opened it to call José in, he was practically bowled over as José came barreling in full-tilt. I had to smile at the look of concern on his small face and how it lit up, seeing me awake. I had the feeling José had not left my side for more than a few seconds in the past two days.

After the doctor had left, José jumped up onto the side of my hospital bed, grinning from ear to ear.

"Shelby, I was so worried about you, but the doc said you were going to be fine. You won't believe it, but I already got me a job and a place to live! Do you remember the little church we brought you to? Pastor David offered me a real job as a maintenance person for the church and stuff. It's so awesome." He grabbed my hand, continuing his gush. "I told him about you looking for your mom and stuff, Shelb's! He's going to try and find them for you. Isn't that wonderful?"

I was a bit overwhelmed by this onslaught and could only manage, "Yeah, José, that's awesome! I'm so happy for you."

"For both of us, Shelby! Everything's going to be okay now...you'll see." I nodded my head and closed my eyes. All I really wanted to do was sleep, but there was one, burning question on my mind.

"Where is Daniel, José?"

José's face fell. He shrugged his shoulders. "I don't know what happened to him, Shelby. He disappeared as soon as we arrived at the church. I haven't seen him since. I'm sorry."

"What are you sorry for?" I asked, holding back the tears.

He didn't answer. He bent his head down solemnly, and I hugged him weakly, ruffling his messy hair. "Where's Oreo?"

José's face lit up. "She's doing great. Pastor David found her a cage and now she has a nice home, too. She's missing you, I can tell," he winked.

"I'm real glad you found a place, José." I meant it with all my heart.

The doctor was true to his word. He sent me over to get x-rays and more blood work. A female nurse came into my room later that day and checked me all over. It was embarrassing, but she said it was something all girls went through. I can't even remember going to a doctor before. I went to the dentist once; I remembered that little experience quite well. I had fallen and broken a tooth and was crying so much Jack finally yelled to my Mamie, "Get that little brat to a dentist before I punch her in the head!" Good times and fond memories, right? Mostly whenever I was sick or hurt, momma just took care of me. She seemed always to have what I needed.

Chapter Twenty-Four

The News

Pastor David drove ten miles over the speed limit in his haste to reach a well-known prominent couple. He pulled into the driveway of a sprawling ranch-style home. He was out the door before the engine completely shut off. His hand shook as he lifted the gold doorknocker, rapping three times in quick succession.

His grin reached from ear to ear as Elizabeth Adams opened her front door.

"Why, Pastor David! What a nice surprise!" She stepped back, "Come in, please."

He walked past her into the main hall and turned around facing her. "Is your husband home, Mrs. Adams?"

"Yes, he's in the den," she motioned to a glass door on the left and led the way as David followed close behind her.

"Honey, Pastor David is here to see you."

"Actually, I'm here to speak with you both."

"Oh! Well, alright then." Elizabeth sidled up to her husband.

Bobbie Adams held out his hand, "Good evening, Pastor. To what do I owe this honor?" Bobbie was tall and lean with archaic features and a Roman nose. His wife was the opposite with long chestnut hair and doll-like features. Combined, they made the perfect couple.

"Please have a seat; you might need to sit down for this. I have something to discuss that concerns you both." Elizabeth and

Bobbie exchanged a concerned look but did as asked. When they both were seated, David began.

"A few days ago, a young girl was brought into the church by her young friend. She was very ill. Jacob and I took her to the hospital, and they ran some tests on her, including a DNA test upon my request. The girl is fourteen years old." He clears his throat.

"Mayor, Mrs. Adams, I believe she is Mary Elizabeth."

Elizabeth stood up; her face is ashen.

"I...I... are you sure? I mean, how do you know for sure?" She turned a pleading eye on her husband. "Bobbie? Can it be true?"

Bobbie Adams stood up next to his wife. "Are you sure, Pastor?"

"It's not one hundred percent positive yet, but I would bet my life on it. We need your DNA to make a positive I.D., the doctor used some of yours from your last lab work, but he said he needed a fresh sample to make sure...but I have no doubt it's her."

"What makes you think it's our Mary beyond a refutable DNA test?" Bobbie's voice was thick with emotion as he asked hoarsely, "What makes you so sure it's our little girl?"

"Because Mayor, she is the spitting image of your wife. Second, she came to the very same church that she was kidnaped from, and third, because the boy who brought her told me she had been kidnaped as a baby, that's why."

The Mayor grabbed his wife before she hit the floor; fainting.

While sitting in his car still in front of the Adam's home, Pastor David called Doctor Morris.

****

141

The next morning, the Doctor held his office door open to a couple walking towards him. He held out his hand when they reached him.

"Mrs. Adams, Mayor Adams, thank you for coming." He preceded them into his office and shut the door behind them. He turned around and smiled. "I have good news. Our mystery girl is, in fact, your daughter." His grin widened as the shock registering on their both their faces.

Elizabeth burst into tears. Bobbie, with tears in his own eyes, enfolded his wife in his arms. Over her head, he asked, "How is this possible, after all this time?"

"You won't believe it, but before I tell you how, there's something you should be aware of. Please have a seat." He motioned to the two chairs in front of his desk. He walked behind his own desk and sat down. He nervously shuffled papers for a moment waiting patiently for Mrs. Adams sobs to quiet down so she could understand him clearly.

"Shelby has been through a lot for a girl her age," Doctor Morris said softly. "After the testing we had done, we discovered she had been physically abused."

Elizabeth's head popped up. "*What?*" The anger on her face shook him to the core.

Bobbie Adams grabbed his wife's hand. "What happened to our little girl, Doc?"

"We took Mary down to x-ray and ran some tests on her. We also did a physical exam." Doctor Morris cleared his throat. This was the part he hated. He always hated giving out bad news, but knew it was his responsibility to give it.

"Her right leg has been broken at some point, my guess by the sloppy mending job about four years ago. Her hip, her pelvic, and her arm have also been broken at one time, or another."

Elizabeth stared at the Doctor, her fists clenching and unclenching. If José had seen her do this, he would know exactly where he had seen this action before. Elizabeth jumped up.

"By WHO?" Her shriek of anger echoed off the walls and bounced back.

Mr. Adams kept his eyes on the doctor, waiting for the rest. He knew there was more. The doctor wasn't finished. He grabbed his wife's hand and pulled her down next to him. "He has something more to tell us." His hands were shaking.

Doctor Morris stood and came around the front of his desk. He half-sat on the edge. "Mary has been sexually assaulted. She has a lot of scar tissue. She'll never be able to carry a child."

They both froze. The doctor could see the stark reality sinking in then out; settling, then coming back like the surge of the surf. Both Bobbie and his wife took a deep breath. Elizabeth swiped at her cheek, wiping the tears away now looking at the Doctor stonily.

"After looking carefully over her chart, I saw the callous formations or a better term, hairline cracks in her bones, where they had been broken at a younger age. She has developed scar tissue or adhesions around her uterus." He looked up and met their eyes. "After she gets settled, I want to run some more tests. Surgery can possibly fix the problem with the scar tissue, but I'm not sure the extent of the damage yet."

Doctor Morris sat his file down on the desk and looked at them both compassionately. "With that being said and out of the way, I want you to know something. Mary is strong! She is brave, and she has traveled over two thousand miles to find you. What she needs now from the both of you is to show her that you love her, no matter what. She doesn't need your pity. She's going to need your help to cope and put this behind her. That will take time...time and love.

"One more thing. After talking with her, I don't believe she can remember much of what happened to her. Her brain has blocked most of it."

Doctor Morris took out a card from his breast pocket and handed it to Elizabeth. "I would like for you to set up an appointment as soon as possible with Doctor Avery. She's the most qualified in her field and works especially with children." At Mrs. Adams questioning look he continued, stating firmly but gently, "She's a psychologist, Mrs. Adams. "Elizabeth pursed her lips. "What about the people who did this?"

"I gave all the information to the police. They'll handle it from here. From what I gathered, the woman who took her died recently. The other, a man, is still out there."

Chapter Twenty-Five
Home

I gaze out the large plate-glass window that's facing a parking lot. The bed I lie in is foreign to me; too soft and comfortable after spending a month upon month on hay, dirt and old blankets either José, Daniel or myself managed to find. I hear the soft whirring of the air conditioner as it kicks on. It pushed cool tempered air into the room, and I marveled over it. A cool breeze at a touch of a button!

I miss Daniel. I wonder why he left me. I just couldn't believe that he would abandon me, but he did. I lowered my head and cried a little. I miss my chicken, too.

I hear the door open and turn toward the sound. A woman and man walk in. A scent of cinnamon follows. I meet her eyes.

I know that the face from somewhere, I think curiously. Her hair is shoulder length and the same color as mine, but with some light gray streaks that seemed to highlight her natural color more than make her look older. I wait...

There it is. She smiled at me. *Yes! Yes!* Her eyes sparkle. I can't speak. I try, but nothing comes out. Instead, I take in a deep breath and let it out slowly. My hands are trembling, but they don't say anything.

Why? What's wrong with me now? I try to lower my eyes in shame and make myself look smaller in my bed, but there's nowhere to go.

I can't take my eyes off her. The handsome man beside her speaks. My eyes dart to him suspiciously. He smiles awkwardly at me. They both shuffle closer to my hospital bed. The man moves forward. His knuckles touch my cheek, making me flinch. His eyes match mine. They are brownish-green in color and so soft.

Oh...they are so soft.

"Mary..." Tears form in his eyes. "I..." he stammers, "I mean we." He looks over at the woman, then back toward me. I watch him warily, waiting to see if he was going to try and touch me again. Something inside me told me it was okay, though.

Something...

"We've missed you so much. I don't know even where to begin." With that, he began to weep.

I still can't speak. My vocal cords have betrayed me. So instead, I timidly reach my hand out. He takes it in his. His bleary gaze softens even more.

Movement catches my eye. The woman moves in. The man lets my hand slip from his. He steps back. She comes closer, taking his place at the side of my bed. She doesn't speak, just looks into my eyes. I see the pain there and something else.

"Mary, I'm so sorry!" She breaks down. She sobs into her hands in braying, unleashed anguish. I could feel her pain coming off of her in waves. I had a sudden urge to make her feel better.

The only thing that comes out of my mouth is, "I love your hair."

The woman stops sobbing and gently takes my hand. I felt something like an electric jolt shoot through me, but pleasant; like something that was twisted in my very soul just unraveled and smoothed out. The woman smiles down at me. "You are so beautiful!"

"She looks just like you," the man said smiling.

I looked up at her as the dawn of realization rushed over me. I gripped her hand tightly, forming the words that took me three tries before they came out.

"Momma, is it you?"

"Yes baby...you made it home.

"You made it home to me."

The world closed it's eyes gently, allowing Shelby her moment with her mother and father. If the world could have stopped spinning, if the skies could have paused their march of clouds, if the very fabric of time could have ceased to exist in those few minutes that followed...they did.

Shelby closed her eyes as her mom and dad hugged her and for the first time in her life; she felt completely safe.

Chapter Twenty-Six

A New Beginning

Three months have passed since I had found my parents. There were days I felt as if I were dreaming. The town had welcomed me and joyfully took me in as one of their own. For the first time in my young life, I felt like I belonged. In one more week, I was to start back to school. I'll be a freshman in high school. I missed the first half, but mom and dad felt it would be best if I rested up before another big change.

José' took to the Pastor like butter spread on bread. The Pastor and his wife were talking about adopting him and were well into the process of hunting down the proper authorities. I was truly happy for him. He deserved some happiness more than anyone else I had ever known.

The police still haven't found Jack. The old house had been abandoned for a while, they said. My parents took care of all the legalities of it. The house was now in my name. They are working with a real-estate firm to try and sell the place and put the money in a college fund. A little part of me still felt the loss of a woman who kidnaped me, and I supposed it always would. I didn't feel anger anymore, though. I felt a great, swelling pity, instead.

I have to go see a special doctor, Mrs. Avery, once a week to help me adjust, (at least that's what she told me) but I know why and its scares me. I don't want to remember but she told me that if I didn't bring the icky stuff to the surface and deal with it, it would always come back in my nightmares where I had no control over them.

I know now that Mamie had taken part in the abuse. I still don't remember a lot of it. The doc said I would eventually remember, and that it was okay.

I hoped not.

I sat on the cold cement bench waiting while my mother ran inside the post office to pay some bills. Even in January, the weather is nice. No snow! Christmas was a bit scary for me. I received a huge amount of gifts. I was still getting used to the idea of even new clothes, much less a laptop computer, an IPod cell phone, a Kindle Fire tablet, my own account to the Amazon bookstore, (my parents found out early my love for books...especially Romance and Christian)

There's a bite to the air. I slip my hands into the pockets of my new red blazer and as always, reflect back on the old Army jacket José had once scrounged for me from the bin of a Goodwill drop box what seemed like years ago.

My eyes scan the surroundings. Goose bumps rise up on my arms. An eerie feeling washes over me. I turn my head and smiled. My heart skips a beat. Moisture fills my eyes.

"Where have you been?" I asked softly, nervously.

Daniel sits next to me and smiled in return. "You didn't need me anymore, Shelby. You," he picked up my hand, "are going to be okay." He rubbed his lips against my palm. "I wanted to say good bye."

"But... where will you go?" My arm tingled. "Will I ever see you again?"

His eyes look past me. "No," he whispered.

"Who are you really?" I asked.

His eyes locked onto mine. "I think you already know."

I nod my head. Yes, I knew. He was my guardian angel sent to guide my way. I leaned in and pressed my lips against his cheek.

"I love you." My voice cracked. "I will always love you," I whispered.

"I know, and I love you." He let my hand drop. "You clean up real good! I knew you were going to turn into a great beauty," he smiled at me. Daniel stood up and glanced down. "Goodbye, my Mary Elizabeth."

I watched him fade away. If it weren't for him, I never would have found my real mom and dad. Everything was going to be okay. He said it. I felt as if my heart was breaking and mending at the same time.

I finally figured out his magic trick to just disappearing.

"Mary, are you ready to go home?" My mother asked when she walked out of the post office.

I stood up and looked down the empty sidewalk and smiled. "Yes, Mom, I'm ready."

Epilogue

I think I found what I wanted to do for a living...or at the least, give it a shot. José had come up to me a few weeks ago and proudly told me that it was his plan to go into the ministry and follow Pastor David's footsteps. As I looked at him, I had to smile. When José said he was going to do something, José was going to do it, no question about it.

"You'll make a great Preacher, big brother." I reached down and hugged him tightly. When I stood up, he straightened on his tiptoes and tussled my hair like I had done his so many times. I laughed.

"Don't I know it!" he winked.

As I sit in my room in front of my laptop, I inspected the blank space; my head already full to bursting. Leaning down, I typed out the title and first line without hesitation:

The Road Is Curved Ahead: Book 2 of Shelby

Chapter One

The beginning

Shelby saw the old church in the distance as the bells sang a warm welcome with their, *ding-dong-ding* chimes...

She typed through the night, her mother and father checking on her once or twice but not disturbing her, knowing that this would only help get the poison out. As she typed though, one thought stayed in the back of her mind like an un-plucked thorn:

Jack is still out there...and it's far from over.

The End

About the Author

Lisa Glenn, born in Montana and raised in Wyoming now resides in the Panhandle of Florida. She is a proud Grandmother of two beauties and a mother of four. Along with her writing, she also works in cover designing, and when she is not writing or working, she is furthering her education at NWFS College. Glenn along with her ten-year-old daughter raise chickens and a Jack Russell/Yorkie mix When Glenn writes, she chugs coffee by the gallons and eats her favorite treat, anything chocolate. She currently is working on her next novel.

Thank you for reading my book, 'Shelby'. Please feel free to leave a review and know that I welcome any and all feedback.

Please keep a look-out for book two in this series coming soon.

Lisa Glenn, October 9th, 2014

Shadowvision1@yahoo.com

lmgshadow1@gmail.com

Twitter: @lisamaeglenn

http://lmgshadow1.wix.com/lisamaeglenn

https://www.facebook.com/pages/Lisa-Glenn/1445107839048590

Now for a sneak peek, coming in February 2015

The Fisherman

1

Kazoo! He hit the solid earth with a loud smack! The ground shook from the vibrations of his landing. Cain shivered. The wetness of the cold snow numbed his backside. His dark shoulder length hair lay frozen against his head. He felt the snowflakes kissing his nose as they fell, cold and wet from the sky. Making sure his toes were still attached he wiggled them. He tried to sit up to no avail. He's frozen. Hades almighty where has he been sent to? He turned his head, letting his gaze roam the area, and with a frown marring his features, he took in the frozen landscape. All he was able to see was a whiteness coating everything, nothing but white snow and the peaks of majestic Mountains in the far distance. The thought of all that snow brought back a sudden flash of memory long buried.

He and his brother had been sitting on the bank of the river, ice-fishing, trying to catch their dinner. He squeezed his eyes shut and pushed back the memory, back to the full dark cell where the memories hidden from a long ago lie. It didn't matter anymore. That time was long past. Why the memory came unbidden to the surface now, he had not a clue.

He tried to think of a time when he had ever been this cold-never. He focused his thoughts to a warm blazing fire, and soon the cold began to ease away to get replaced with the warmth of a bright summer day. The ground around his body melted into a clear liquid, to seep into the once frozen ground. Ah, much better. He stretched his large muscles and sat up. Not knowing what direction he needed to take, he stuck his finger up

154

into the brisk air and waited for a slight breeze to guide him. When the breeze tickled his finger, he decided east would be a great place to start. Naked, he stood up. He began to walk, the snow melting as each foot touched the snow covered ground. By the look of it, he had a ways to go. He squinted off into the distance and wasn't able to see a single structure, the glare off the snow causing his eyes to water. He would use this time to think up a plan. He was thinking of all the fun he was about to be engaged as he smiled widened. He loved this part of his job, chaos…and sin. Yes, he was looking forward to that part the best-sin

2

"He is such a Creep! I can't believe he did it again. If I had a lick of sense, I wouldn't let him see her. She doesn't deserve this crap!"

"Liza, you can't do that to her. She loves her dad." Margaret stood at the stove stirring the stew as it bubbled, letting out a tantalizing aroma.

"Mom, he's never around enough for her to know him let alone love the man. He calls her every other month and only drops in when he is looking for money. Don't you think that hurts her? I am tired of watching her in pain because of him! He hasn't paid any child support in over a year! She needs more than that from a father. How many times has he not showed up when he said he would? I would love it if he'd just stay away for good!" Liza replied, drawing in a shaky breath.

She stood in front of a large bay window looking out at the snow-covered mountains in the distance. She hated this time of year; Cold and dreary. Missy was in the yard building a snowman, twice the size of her small 4 foot frame. It wasn't her daughter's fault the creep was never around, yet she was the one suffering. Her daughter was the one bright light in Liza's dark existence. Giving her Missy was the only good thing Joe had ever done for her.

Liza married Joe Marsh after they both had graduated from high school. Soon after the wedding and three months after Missy was born,

Joe had walked out. A year later they were divorced. Now nine years later, at 29 Liza still hadn't forgiven him. He had left her with a new baby. Unable to support herself and Missy, she had to move in with her mother. Liza loved her mother and was pleased it had worked out this way, but she still hated Joe.

Her mom was dying of cancer, and now Liza was able to take care of her like she had taken care of them. Every day it was getting harder not to break down and scream and cry out for the injustice of it all. Some days she felt like she didn't deserve what God put before her and yet other days she felt as if she was well deserved of it. From the time, she'd hit her teens she has been driving her mother through the ringer, from one scrape to another.

Her father had passed away when Liza had been very young. She didn't remember much about him. Aunt Tobey, her father's sister, often came to visit. She would tell Liza things about her father that her mother didn't know she knew. He had been excessively abusive cheating on her mother more than once. When he had taken ill and right before he died, he had confessed all his sins to Aunt Tobey, asking for forgiveness.

It didn't come as a great surprise to Liza; she knew something was up when her mother never spoke of him. They never spoke about him.

Her mother had always been the one great fixture in her life. When she had been around 11 or 12 her mother had come to the school yet again to pick her up for fighting but instead of yelling at her she took her out for ice cream. She kept out of trouble after that, at least until her junior year of High School. Her mother had been called in again, this time for blackening another class mate's eye during P.E. She got her car taken away for a month that time.

Liza never dated, although the men asked. She was pretty in a girl-next-door kind of way. Her strawberry blonde hair cut short framed her pixie-like features. Her eyes small and blue in color sported long eyelashes. She was of medium height with a slender build. The problem wasn't in the way she looked it was the fact that she hated all men. From what she had seen and what she had experienced for herself, Liza didn't want one. She didn't need one. They were all troublesome from her point of view. Her mother was always trying to speak sense into her.

Turning from the partially frosted window, Liza turned toward her mother. "Mom, I don't want to talk about him anymore. Let's change this subject. Missy is coming in anyway."

Margaret signed, "I just want what's best for you both. I wish you didn't carry this anger inside. It's not healthy. Liza you need to forgive and forget. He isn't worth all this anger. It's not good for Missy either."

She pursed her lips, "I can't Mom, and the anger is what keeps me going. Every day, every moment of every day, I have a deep seeded desire to kill him..." The sound of the door opening ceased all talk.

"Mom, Grandma, come look at Frosty!" Missy walked in all bundled up in her down jacket and bright yellow knit hat with matching mittens. "Hey Grandma, can I have a carrot for his nose? Whatta ya got for a hat? That's all I need to make him perfect."

Margaret chuckled, "right now dinner is ready. We'll go have a look after dinner. You need to warm up some. Your nose is the color of Rudolph's!"

"Ah Grandma." Missy shrugged her coat off and left it lying on the floor next to the door.

Liza sauntered into the kitchen, "You heard her Missy! Go wash up and hurry, you can set the table." She ushered her mother over to the kitchen table, "Mom, sit while I finish this up."

"Don't forget the muffins in the oven, and I made some tea; the pitcher is in the fridge," Margaret said as she wearily sat down to wait on her two girls.

"Mom I got this. You relax." Liza grabbed a set of oven mitts out of the top kitchen drawer and slid them over her hands. She opened up the oven door and pulled out the sourdough biscuits. She set the hot pan on the counter, and one by one placed the hot biscuits onto an oval dish to be served. She turned as Missy came into the room. "Missy will you set the table while I ladle up the stew?" She grabbed three large bowls down from the cupboard and from the large pot filled each one to the brim with steaming flavorful stew. Missy took each bowl as they were filled and set them on the table.

"Mm...mm, Grams this sure smells good!" Missy sat down and waited beside her Grandma. Her stomach grumbled as the smell drifted lazily from the pot.

Liza sat down at the table, "Alright everyone, let's eat." She picked up her spoon, the smell of the biscuits' making her mouth water.

"Wait, we forgot to," Margaret said halting Missy's progress, spoon to mouth.

Liza winked at Missy then rolled her eyes, "Yeah, okay Mom." Her mom thought she needed to pray at every meal, to thank God for the food. Liza thought it was a waste of time. Why thank him? He sure didn't cook it! Liza remembered a long time ago when she had been 7 or 8 years old she had believed, but that was all in her past. What kind of God would make her mom sick? Make this life so hard? She shook her head at the humor of it all. Her mother believed, so Liza kept her negative remarks to a minimal.

"Dear heavenly Father, thank you for this food we are about to eat, may it nourish our bodies...and Lord, please help my daughter, she is going to need it. Amen." Missy started to giggle. Margaret grinned.

Liza groaned, "Very funny, Mom."

Knock, knock, knock. They all three glanced over at the front door. Liza looked up and met her mother's eyes. She stood up. *Finely.* Maybe Joe decided to sober up enough to see his daughter. Liza threw the napkin down onto the table. She walked over to the door and without looking through the peephole to see who it was; she opened it ready to give Joe a piece of her mind. Instead, she gasped! Her mouth fell open. *Wow!* A man stood in the doorway. A very large naked, gorgeous man!

57320951R00096

Made in the USA
Charleston, SC
10 June 2016